Avec Schmaltz

by Mart Crowley

SAMUEL FRENCH

FOUNDED 1830

NEW YORK HOLLYWOOD LONDON TORONTO

SAMUELFRENCH.COM

ISBN 978-0-573-60076-0   Printed in U.S.A.   #29733

MUSIC USE NOTE

Licensees are solely responsible for obtaining formal written permission from copyright owners to use copyrighted music in the performance of this play and are strongly cautioned to do so. If no such permission is obtained by the licensee, then the licensee must use only original music that the licensee owns and controls. Licensees are solely responsible and liable for all music clearances and shall indemnify the copyright owners of the play and their licensing agent, Samuel French, Inc., against any costs, expenses, losses and liabilities arising from the use of music by licensees.

IMPORTANT BILLING AND CREDIT REQUIREMENTS

All producers of *AVEC SCHMALTZ* *must* give credit to the Author of the Play in all programs distributed in connection with performances of the Play, and in all instances in which the title of the Play appears for the purposes of advertising, publicizing or otherwise exploiting the Play and/or a production. The name of the Author *must* appear on a separate line on which no other name appears, immediately following the title and *must* appear in size of type not less than fifty percent of the size of the title type.

AVEC SCHMALTZ was originally performed (in an earlier version) under the title *THE SPIRIT OF IT ALL* on August 11, 1984, in The New Play Series at the Williamstown Theatre Festival, Williamstown, MA. (Nicos Psacharopoulous, Artistic Director). The play was directed by Steve Lawson. The cast was as follows:

KIT	Marsha Mason
NELLIE	Erica Auerbach
JOSH	Kiefer Sutherland
NICK	Frank Hankey
MANNY	James Naughton
WENDY	Wendy Kahn
COLIN	Kevin Spacey

CHARACTERS

KIT – Mid-30s, beautiful, flame-haired, "well-finished" private school girl, divorced mother of a young daughter and teenage son.

NELLIE – 7 year-old freckled miniature of her mother, feisty, glib.

JOSH – 15 year-old, dark-eyed, dark-haired, smart, sensitive, droll.

NICK – Mid-30s, handsome, polished, divorced WASP "rich-boy."

MANNY – Mid-30s, attractive, jokey, Jewish ex-rock musician turned television composer, ex-husband of Kit and father of Nellie and Josh.

WENDY – Late-20s, sexy, savvy TV producer.

COLIN – Mid-30s, nice-looking, well-educated, sophisticated professional violinist.

SETTING

Act One: Christmas Eve at a farmhouse in rural Connecticut.
Act Two: New Year's Eve at a home in Beverly Hills, California.

For Glynnis and Marty [Mr. & Mrs. Mark Snow]

ACT I

(The living room of a Connecticut farm which might be characterized as "under glass." The architecture is dreamhouse American colonial – the ambiance, magazine cover charm. It's about seven p.m. and the room is cheerful with holiday decorations.)

(The front door is upstage in the right wall; when it is opened a wreath of holly can be seen, hanging around a brass knocker. Up center are the stairs which have an evergreen garland, scalloped up the banister. Beneath the stairs is a short closet door. Up center left of the stairs is an open French armoire which serves as a bar, generously stocked with liquor, tumblers, and stemware. On a middle shelf there is a big crystal pitcher of eggnog and an open bottle of white wine in an ice bucket. Up left of the armoire is a swinging door to the kitchen.)

(The left wall has floor to ceiling bookshelves on either side of a stone fireplace which, at present, is not lighted. Two empty needlepoint stockings hang from the mantel. Upstage of the hearth there is a comfortable overstuffed chair with a loose faded chintz slipcover. A rustic table with a tolle Chinese tea canister lamp is beside it. On the downstage side of the table is a Windsor chair.)

(Off center left, angled toward the fireplace is a sofa with a matching slipcover. In front of it, a butler's tray "coffee table" with a silver cigarette box and striker, filled with kitchen matches. There is also a large spherical bowl with goldfish swimming in it. Behind the sofa is a rustic French desk and chair. On the desk is a telephone and a brass student's lamp.)

(Overhead center is an old lantern under which a branch of mistletoe is tied with a brilliant red bow.)

(In the left wall there is a large bay window with a semi-circular seat, heaped with colorfully wrapped presents. Standing in the curve of the window is a tall tree, presently being trimmed by **KIT** *and* **JOSH** *and* **NELLIE**.*)*

*(***KIT** *is mid-thirties with strikingly lovely features and glorious red hair. She's dressed in a loose, man's plaid work shirt over a turtleneck and jeans. She wears thick, wooly sox without shoes.* **JOSH** *is a handsome boy of fifteen with dark eyes and dark hair.* **NELLIE** *is seven and has her mother's fair complexion and flaming curls. Both kids have on winter country apparel.)*

*(***KIT** *is on a stepladder, stringing ropes of popcorn onto the tree.* **NELLIE** *is by the coffee table, feeding the goldfish in the bowl.* **JOSH** *is seated at the desk, reading a book. It's a very pretty picture. It could be a Hallmark card or a window in Bloomingdale's.)*

KIT. Well? Anybody here conscious? It can't be the triptophan, we haven't had the turkey yet. *(after a moment)* Well…can I have *some* kind of response?

NELLIE. *(looks up from fishbowl, loudly)* Beautifulfabulousgreat!!

KIT. *(laughs)* Now, that's more like it!

NELLIE. Don't ask me to spell it.

KIT. I'll just settle for a little approval, Nellie, dear. *(looks at* **JOSH***)* I'm afraid your brother doesn't seem to share your opinion.

NELLIE. What's the matter, Joshie, don't you like it?

JOSH. *(not looking up; glumly)* It's okay.

KIT. That good, huh? Not beautifulfabulousgreat?

JOSH. *(gets up, crosses to* **KIT***)* I think it was more *human* last Christmas. This year it seems – how shall I put it – so resolutely "happy hands at home."

*(***KIT***'s expressions slides. She comes down the ladder.)*

KIT. *(glares at* **JOSH***)* Come on. You get up there. These "happy hands" have – how shall I put it – so resolutely *had* it!

(She dumps the popcorn ropes into JOSH*'s arms.)*

JOSH. *(groans)* Oh, god, must we behave as if we're in the colorized version of *It's A Wonderful Life?*

(KIT *raises an eyebrow as* **JOSH** *reluctantly mounts the ladder.* **NELLIE** *crosses to kneel on the window seat and look outside at the falling snow.* **KIT** *finally crosses to the coffee table, takes a cigarette out of a box, starts to light it with a kitchen match from a striker, stops, thinks better of it, blows out the match and returns the cigarette to the box.)*

NELLIE. If you go to all the trouble to put them out in boxes and to play with them, why don't you smoke them?

KIT. *(dryly)* I get a sense of satisfaction out of not being able to enjoy one.

*(*NELLIE *and* JOSH *just stare at her.)*

– Well, it's an answer. I know it makes no sense, but it's an answer.

JOSH. *(after a moment)* Mom…when he gets here – do I have to kiss him?

KIT. *(tries to appear unruffled)* Well…I think that would be very…appropriate….

JOSH. Really?

KIT. Yes, I do. I think that would be a very warm and welcoming thing for a son to…

NELLIE. *(interrupting, crossing to the tree)* Don't put the angel on, Josh! That's what I get to do! Right, Mom?

KIT. Right… *(to* JOSH*)* After all, you haven't seen him since the summer and, in spite of what you may think, your father loves you very much.

JOSH. That's just it, though.

KIT. *(tonelessly)* What's just it, though?

JOSH. I don't know if *I* love *him.*

(Silence. KIT *can't or doesn't choose to speak. Not so,* NELLIE…*)*

NELLIE. Well, I'm going to kiss him! Not so much because I love him especially, but because I love kissing!

JOSH. *(to* **KIT***)* Can you imagine what she's going to be like by the time she gets her period?

KIT. *(annoyed)* Joshua, really! I've asked you repeatedly to please not…

JOSH. She doesn't understand.

KIT. That's not for you to decide and that's hardly the point!

JOSH. Okay, okay, I'm sorry!

NELLIE. *(to* **JOSH***)* And I understand. And I'm going to sing to him, too!
(*bellowing)* "SI-E-LENT NIGHT…HO-O-LEE NIGHT…"

JOSH. YOU'RE SUPPOSED TO SING "SILENT NIGHT" *SILENTLY*!!

NELLIE. THEN HOW COULD YOU *HEAR* IT?! THAT'S DUMB!

KIT. Shhhshhh!…quiet!…Your brother means *softly*, sweetheart. *(musically)* You should sing it *softly*.

NELLIE. *(quickly, to* **KIT***)* I love Daddy even if Josh doesn't!

JOSH. *(loudly)* I never said I *didn't*, I said I didn't *know*!

(He snatches at a rope of popcorn which shakes the limbs, causing some of the ornaments to clatter. **NELLIE** *screams.)*

NELLIE. NO, NO! YOU'RE RUINING IT! STOP IT, STOP IT!!

JOSH. WILL YOU SHUT UP?!!

*(***KIT** *sticks her fingers in her mouth and whistles loudly. The kids quiet.)*

KIT. *(crossing to center)* TIME OUT! Back to your corners! Or should I say, cages! *(softly, to* **NELLIE***)* Ready to put the angel on top, sweetie?

NELLIE. *(excitedly; then, for* **JOSH***'s sake)* I'm ready to bust some bozo's nose!

JOSH. That would be me.

KIT. Now, now, Nell. *(to* **JOSH**, *re: ladder)* Come on, down, Josh. It's time for *It's A Wonderful Life*, The Sequel.

(JOSH *comes down the ladder and goes to slump into the Windsor chair.* **NELLIE** *mounts the ladder,* **KIT** *minding her.)*

NELLIE. I just love Christmas! It's so red and green!

(KIT *smiles.* **NELLIE** *takes the angel and places it on top of the tree.)*

NELLIE. There! How does she look?

KIT. *(softly, looking at* **NELLIE**) She looks…beautiful, fabulous, great…

NELLIE. *(privately, to* **KIT**) I hope Daddy thinks so, too.

(NELLIE *comes down the ladder into* **KIT**'s *arms.)*

KIT. *(kissing* **NELLIE** *on the cheek)* He will, darling. I know he will.

JOSH. He doesn't like Christmas at all. He's Jewish.

(KIT *sets* **NELLIE** *down, turns to* **JOSH**, *fed up.)*

KIT. *(flatly)* He likes Christmas just fine! He just never celebrated it as a child so it doesn't mean that much to him. But he likes it…*evah* so much! *(turns to* **NELLIE**, *sweetly)* Especially angels. *(to* **JOSH**, *through her teeth)* And *we're* going to like it, too!

JOSH. *(groans loudly)* Oh, it's some wonderful fucking life, all right!

KIT. *Joshua!* I will not have you using such thoroughly appalling…

JOSH. SOR-*REEEE*!!

NELLIE. Are you gonna kiss him when he gets here, Mommie?

KIT. *(lightly)* Don't I always when he comes to see us?

(KIT *"nonchalantly" hangs the remainder of the ornaments on the tree.)*

JOSH. *(grimly)* You kiss him on the cheek.

KIT. *(with an edge)* Well, *that's kissing*, is it not?

NELLIE. *(hanging an ornament)* You kiss Nick on the mouth.

JOSH. Yeah. Great big wet toilet plungers.

KIT. *(to JOSH, dryly)* Exquisitely put.

(**JOSH** *makes a rude popping sound with his lips.* **KIT** *throws a Christmas ball at him.* **JOSH** *is pleased to get a rise out of her.*)

NELLIE. Does that mean you love Nick and you don't love Daddy anymore?

KIT. *(with a certain "great lady" air)* No, that does *not* necessarily mean that I love Nick at all. Though I do love him in a *certain* way – which is not to say that I don't still love your father in a *certain* way, too, but…well, we *are* divorced and although I will always have a *certain* kind of…well, *loving feeling* for him, it's certainly not at all what I feel for Nick, whether you call it love or not. Does that make sense?

NELLIE. *Certainly not.*

JOSH. Yeah, Mom, it needs work. And I don't mean the tree.

(**KIT** *gives them both a look, sighs with a modicum of defeat.*)

NELLIE. Is that why you're not still married? Is it because Daddy doesn't love you anymore?

KIT. You'll have to ask *him* that.

NELLIE. Is it because he loves Wendy now?

KIT. You'll have to ask him that, too.

JOSH. I bet he doesn't kiss *her* on the cheek. I bet he gives her a big wet…Well – something *e*xquisitely put.

NELLIE. He gives her jewelry, too. Well, I guess he does. She's got it, anyway. I saw it in the picture he sent. The blurry one where everything looks like stars, including the middles of her eyes.

KIT. *Everybody* named Wendy has jewelry.

NELLIE. Not in *Peter Pan.* Of course, that Wendy's wearing a nightgown, so it could be in the vault.

(**NELLIE** *drapes a rope of popcorn around her neck as if they were pearls.* **JOSH** *catches* **KIT***'s eye…*)

JOSH. My sister, the material midget. I'll bet she's gonna have jewels. Big, *angry* jewels like Grandma Corinne.

NELLIE. I'm *not* a midget! I'm petite. Grandma Corinne says so!

(**KIT** *freezes at the mention of the name.*)

KIT. Come on, Nell, you've got to be in bed so Santa Claus can come.

NELLIE. There ain't no Santa Claus.

KIT. Oh, there ain't, ain't there? Where'd you get that idea, as-if-I-didn't-know.

(**KIT** *looks at* **JOSH***.*)

JOSH. I never said a word!

KIT. *(calmly, to* **NELLIE***)* Go on up and get started with your bath – I'll be there in a minute. Not too much water.

NELLIE. I hope you're gonna say something to Josh about his language.

(**KIT** *glares at* **NELLIE***…* **NELLIE** *goes to* **JOSH***, throws her arms about his neck…*)

(*too adorably*) 'Night, 'night, Joshie darling.

JOSH. Bitch.

(**KIT** *gives him a barely tolerant look, scoots* **NELLIE** *up the stairs, laughing "wickedly." After she is out of sight,* **KIT** *and* **JOSH** *lock eyes.*)

I *never* said a word! Besides, do you honestly think she doesn't…

KIT. *(matter-of-fact)* Well, I hope not. It's probably the last Christmas she'll even *wonder* about *anything*! Where babies come from. Whether there's a God or not. And, oh, God, Josh, I *do* wish you wouldn't use such unnecessary, ghastly…

JOSH. I know, I know. What I said just slipped out.

KIT. Well, try to get a little more traction on the four-letter words.

JOSH. Yeah, yeah.

KIT. And I wish you'd get a little yuletide spirit! It wouldn't kill you to go along with things for a little while.

(**KIT** *takes a cardboard box which the decorations were in and begins to deposit the clutter in it...* **JOSH** *goes to the stepladder, folds it, stops...*)

JOSH. Mom, is he gonna sleep with you?

KIT. Who, Santa Claus?

JOSH. You know who I mean.

KIT. He's going to sleep in the guest room like last time.

(**JOSH** *takes the ladder to the closet beneath the stairs, puts it inside.*)

JOSH. I guess Nick won't be staying overnight as long as *he's* here.

KIT. *(mildly irritated)* Nick has never stayed overnight in this house ever, and you know it!

JOSH. But you do sleep with him, don't deny it.

KIT. *("grandly" defensive) Not in this house!*

JOSH. At his place? Or in motels?

KIT. Just in motels. Just in wretched little fleabag motels. And when one isn't available, the odd sordid flophouse.

JOSH. How does Nick compare to Dad? In the sack, I mean.

(**KIT** *stops, puts down the box, faces* **JOSH** *directly.*)

KIT. *(evenly)* Look, I don't like this conversation. I don't like your smutty, smug impudence – the relentless way you've been trying your best to spoil this holiday.

(**JOSH** *turns away from her.*)

I know we've been having a rocky time lately. Are you furious at me and your father because we broke up? Because we wrecked something for *you?* Well, I can understand that. It was a big disappointment for us, too. A *very* big one. And it wasn't anybody's fault but your father's and mine. Not your's. Not Nell's. Just the two people who happen to be your parents. The two people who happen to love you the most!

(A moment, then **JOSH** *hurls a box of ornaments across the room and runs upstairs.* **KIT** *releases a deep sigh, slowly goes to pick up the scattered ornaments. The phone rings, she moves to the desk to answer it...)*

KIT. Hello? *(dully)* Oh, hello, Mother. Ohh...decorating. I was just watching Josh finish off the ornaments. Yes, the tree's lovely. Maybe a tad too "Hallmark card-ish" this year but... No, nothing's the matter, I'm fine – is it snowing in the city? The weather man on TV said it might. I don't know which one – just somebody with a good haircut in front of one of those big, swirling maps which are fascinating but tell you nothing. *(She picks up the instrument, brings it around to the sofa and sinks back in its cushions.)* No, nary a flake here, neither. Oh? Is that a double negative? Sorry. No, he hasn't arrived and I haven't heard from him. No, I haven't heard from Linda, yet, either – *neither*? I don't know what's correct but no calls from Paris. But you know how that goes with my dear sister... Yes, mother, I know she's a very, very busy person with very, very important things on her mind like the fate of the world and all, but...no, I'm not being catty and, yes, I *do* have the Christmas spirit. Listen, what time are you coming tomorrow? Oh, I don't know, I suppose we'll eat around four so come anytime you like...*after three.* Is Lucky driving you up or did you give him the day off? Oh. *(suddenly sits bolt upright)* No, Mother, *don't*! I do not need any extra help so *do not* bring Rolando and Arlene! Didn't you let them off, either? *Neither* one of them – I mean, *none* of them? They must all have the Christmas spirit, too! *(change of tone)* Oh, so sorry – no, for heaven's sake don't let me keep you! Whose party? Un, well, give everyone at Gracie Mansion my seasons greetings. Yeah, see you tomorrow... *(quickly)*

– and Mother, please…*one* request in advance: *(takes a deep breath, then rattles off a litany)* Try to like my hair, my clothes, my children's hair and clothes, my house, my hospitality and my ex-husband. No, I'm not trying to be snide, I'm just trying to *lay it on the line for you.* Yeah, have a good time at the Mayor's. Uh-huh, to you, too. *(She hangs up, says to herself through clenched teeth…)* I hate her. Oh, god, how I hate her.

*(**KIT** reaches for the cigarette box on the coffee table, opens it, removes one, stops, thinks, tosses it back into the box, thinks…suddenly picks up the whole box and crosses to the fireplace to throw the entire contents onto the hearth.)*

NELLIE. Building a fire?

*(**KIT** looks up to see **NELLIE** leaning over the banister, wearing a nightgown which could be out of Peter Pan.)*

KIT. Yes, darling, with Mommie's old cigarettes.

*(**KIT** strikes a match and lights the little pile, picks up a poker. **NELLIE** descends the stairs.)*

NELLIE. You've been doing real good. Those patches seem to work – but they aren't very pretty.

KIT. You don't see them under my clothes.

NELLIE. I know. But I know they're there. *(She crosses to **KIT**.)* Are we going to light the tree?

KIT. *(not letting the last remark faze her)* We sure are, but we have to call Joshie first. My, my, don't you smell divine.

NELLIE. *(sheepishly)* I cheated and opened my present from Grandma Corinne. Bath oil. Gardenia. I knew it would be.

KIT. *(grimly)* Mmmm, you seem to know an awful lot of stuff. Well, thank her when she comes tomorrow and be sure to write her a little note, too. That means a lot to her. Like the difference between life and death.

*(**KIT** pokes hostilely at the fire and it flames up.)*

NELLIE. Grandma Corinne says I take after her.

KIT. *(bluntly)* Don't even *think* it!

(The doorbell rings.)

NELLIE. *(runs toward the front door)* Oh, Daddy's home! Daddy's home!

*(**KIT** straightens, replaces the poker and crosses to the front door, nervously smoothing her hair. She pulls the front door open to reveal **NICK**. He's about her age, very handsome, dressed in a good business suit, a cashmere overcoat, and silk scarf. His arms are full of presents.)*

KIT. Oh, Nick, it's you! We thought you were an ex-husband but we'll settle.

NICK. Is that a compliment? I can't tell.

NELLIE. Hiya, Uncle Nick!

KIT. Looks more like *Saint* Nick, I'd say. Here, let me help you.

NELLIE. You're looking mighty handsome.

NICK. Well, thanks. *(to **KIT**)* Someone wouldn't be softening me up for their present, would they?

KIT. *(sardonically)* Whatever would give you that idea? It's just an evening of *relentless* good cheer, that's all.

*(**NELLIE** has intervened to take a couple of packages and go to put them under the tree. **KIT** searches the darkness outside the house before closing the front door. **NICK** moves into the room.)*

KIT. *(to **NICK**)* Want a drink? There's eggnog and white wine and…

NICK. Wine sounds good.

NELLIE. Want some fruit cake? We have some left from last year.

NICK. No, thanks.

NELLIE. I'd hate to drop it on my toe.

*(**KIT** has gone to the armoire to pour the wine into a stem glass.)*

KIT. Bourbon or brandy will soften it up.

NELLIE. Soften it, maybe, but not sell it.

KIT. *Sell* it? You can't *give* fruit cake away. Why is that?

NICK. *(shrugs)* I don't know, but even drunks don't want it.

KIT. *(brings* **NICK** *the drink)* I thought you had to play Santa at the club tonight.

NICK. So I'll be a little late. *(takes the drink, gives* **KIT** *the remainder of the presents)* Thanks. I wanted to play Santa here first.

NELLIE. Hooray for our side!

(The swinging door pops open and **JOSH** *enters.)*

JOSH. *(bluntly)* There *is* no Santa Claus, didn't you hear?

NELLIE. YES THERE IS!!

KIT. Quiet, Nell! *(to* **NICK**, *irritated by* **JOSH**) You've met my son, Ebaneezer somebody.

NICK. *(holding out a hand)* Merry Christmas, Josh.

*(***JOSH*** does not shake hands. ***NICK*** self-consciously puts his hand in his pocket.)*

JOSH. *(to* **NICK**) Are you spending the night?

KIT. *(levelly)* If you can't be civil, Josh, be good enough to leave us in peace.

JOSH. *(continuing to* **NICK**) Tonight might not be a good night to stay. We're expecting someone. And I *don't* mean down the chimney.

NICK. Yes, I thought your dad might have arrived already.

NELLIE. You never can be too sure with the Christmas rush, you know.

KIT. *(amused by* **NELLIE**'s *remark)* Come on, Nell, time for bed.

NELLIE. *(petulantly)* But I have to stay up to see Daddy!

KIT. *(dryly)* Well, with the Christmas rush he may have to come on skates. You can see him in the morning.

NELLIE. But I'm not at all sleepy.

KIT. When are you ever? You're the original party girl! I wonder who you get that from?

NICK. Your mother probably.

KIT. *(to* **NICK***)* I had a sinking feeling you were going to say that.

JOSH. Well, Nell certainly doesn't get it from you.

KIT. *(indulgently)* Heavens, no, I'm just old "Happy-Hands-At-Home," the shut-in.

NELLIE. Nick, when are you going to take me sailing on your ship?

NICK. *(pleasantly)* In the spring, if you like. But you don't call it a ship, Nell, you call it a sloop.

NELLIE. Oh. Does it have a living room?

NICK. Uh-huh, but you call that the cabin.

NELLIE. And a kitchen?

NICK. *(nods, laughs)* Uh-huh, but you call that the galley.

NELLIE. *(thinks, after a moment)* What do you call a tomato on a boat?

*(***NICK*** is nonplussed, stops laughing.* **KIT** *laughs. Even* **JOSH** *snickers.)*

KIT. *(to* **NELLIE***)* Say goodnight to Nick.

*(***NICK*** bends to one knee.* **NELLIE** *goes to him, puts her arms around his neck, kisses him on the mouth.* **NICK** *is chagrinned.)*

NELLIE. Goodnight, old Nick. Is my present expensive?

JOSH. Little bitch!

*(***KIT*** takes* **NELLIE** *by the hand…)*

KIT. *(re:* **JOSH***'s remark)* If the charm gets too thick in here, there's an ax in the woodbin.

*(***KIT*** takes* **NELLIE** *up the stairs. When they are out of sight,* **NICK** *turns to* **JOSH***.)*

NICK. Now, come on, Josh, don't tell me you don't have the Christmas spirit?

JOSH. Oh, we've got the Christmas spirit by the gallon. But *you* seem to be fresh out. Let me fill you up again.

*(***JOSH*** takes* **NICK***'s empty wine glass from him, goes to the armoire, pours him another.* **NICK** *eyes him curiously.)*

JOSH. *(cont.)* How come your first marriage failed?

NICK. *(smoothly)* Married the wrong girl, I guess.

JOSH. Now you've found the right one.

> (**JOSH** *crosses to* **NICK** *with his refilled glass, hands it to* **NICK**.)

NICK. *(takes drink)* Thanks. I think so. And I hope she feels the same.

JOSH. How would you like it being our father, Nick?

NICK. How would *you* like it?

JOSH. You go first.

NICK. *(without hesitation)* I'd like it. Your turn.

> (**NICK** *takes a big swallow of wine, watches* **JOSH**.)

JOSH. Well…Grandmother would *really* like it. "Old money," WASP, all the right cliques and all the right clubs. "Good goods," is how she refers to you. Did you know that? Did you know you were "good goods."

NICK. You didn't answer my question.

JOSH. *(bluntly)* I think you want to marry my mother but I think you'd prefer it if she didn't have us – my sister and me. I don't think you really give a shit about the two of us, no matter how many presents you bring. Now, in answer to your question…

> (**KIT** *comes down the stairs.* **NICK** *and* **JOSH** *turn toward her…*)

KIT. She's like something shot out of a cannon – going to be awake all night. We'll have to be extra quiet putting out the toys… *(realizes…)* Oh, am I stepping on the punchline?

NICK. The one before you came in had the wallop.

> (**JOSH** *starts for the stairs.* **KIT** *has reached the bottom and catches him in her arms and hangs on to him for a moment, even though* **JOSH** *resists and pulls away.*)

KIT. Hey, where're you going? We don't want privacy.

JOSH. *I* do. I've got presents to wrap.

KIT. Well, bring them down when you're finished and put them under the tree. I'm counting on you to help me out with the toys. You know I never know Tab A from Slot B.

JOSH. You're Slot A, he's Tab B. Any kid can figure that out.

(**JOSH** *starts to run up the stairs.*)

NICK. Josh.

(**JOSH** *stops.*)

(*directly, but gently*) You have every right to be suspicious of me, but that just isn't true – what you said. I'm *very* fond of you. And Nellie, too. More than you know. I hope you believe that. I want to try and be a good father to you both.

(**JOSH** *doesn't respond, turns and runs up the rest of the stairs and off.* **KIT** *looks at* **NICK** *quickly, goes over to the fireplace, stokes the fire which is now burning beautifully.*)

KIT. I don't even want to think what all of that was about.

NICK. I'm afraid he feels that if we get married, it will officially put an end to his ever having Manny as a father.

KIT. (*flatly*) I thought that was what that was about.

NICK. Josh doesn't think I like him and Nellie – that I only want you and they'll be left out in the cold. That isn't true. You know it isn't.

KIT. (*distressed*) I know, Nick. Oh, I know.

NICK. Of, course, I botched it the first time, but there were reasons. And thank god, there weren't any kids to suffer from my mistakes.

KIT. I botched it, too, the first time – and, I'm afraid, there *are* kids to suffer from my mistakes.

NICK. It couldn't have been all your fault.

(**NICK** *puts down his wine glass, crosses to her.*)

Darling…this may be the last few minutes of the holiday we have together. I want to give you my present – (*takes a small plush box from his pocket*) Now, please don't say, "Oh, Nick, you shouldn't have."

(He hands her the box. She goes to take it, but when she sees what kind of a box it is, she draws her hand back as if it were red hot.)

KIT. *(grimly)* Oh, Nick, you shouldn't have.

NICK. You don't even know what it is!

KIT. I know mittens don't come in a tiny plush box.

NICK. It's not a ring, if that's what you think.

KIT. *(brightly)* Oh, it's not? What is it?

NICK. Just a little trimming of my own, you'll be relieved to know. Open it.

*(**KIT** opens the box.)*

KIT. *(dazzled, gaily)* Oh, Nick, you really shouldn't have but I'm *sooo* glad you did! They're absolutely exquisite! The most beautiful earrings I've ever seen!

NICK. They were my mother's. My father gave them to her at Christmas time, too – when he asked her to marry him.

KIT. *(Her face slides.)* Ohhh, you really shouldn't have.

NICK. *(re: the earrings)* Put them on, Kit. I want you to have them. I can wait. I'm good at that. I've waited a long time. Put them on. Please.

KIT. *(puts her head in her hands)* Oh, I'm so confused, Nick. About so many things. About Manny. About me. You. Us.

NICK. I know you are. But I love you, Kit. I honestly am in love with you. And I think it's for always.

KIT. *(sincerely)* Nick, you're such a fine man. You're thoughtful and attentive and generous and…well, decent. And you don't hardly meet none of them no more.

NICK. "Good goods." Isn't that what Corinne calls me?

KIT. You're better than that. Much better than anything my mother would ever take you for. So good, in fact, I know we could make it work. I know I'd work at making it work.

NICK. That doesn't sound like much fun – all that work.

KIT. Oh, Nick, don't say another syllable. Not tonight. I don't want to spoil it. I don't even know what it is I don't want to spoil, but I know I don't want to do it tonight. It's just that I'm…

NICK. Still in love with him.

KIT. …confused.

(**NICK** *nods understandingly.* **KIT** *takes the earrings out of the box and he helps her put them on. She puts her arms about his neck.*)

(*They kiss. A moment…and the swinging door to the kitchen is pushed open and* **MANNY** *enters. He's in his late thirties with a lean, athletic body, dark eyes and dark hair. He has a decidedly impish quality, something devilishly attractive about him. He is dressed in cords and an expensive sweater and car coat. He has a duffel bag slung over his shoulder.*)

MANNY. Pardon me, but aren't you suppose to be standing under the mistletoe for that sort of thing?

(**KIT** *and* **NICK** *break apart, startled.*)

KIT. Manny!

MANNY. I guess you might say you *missed* the mistletoe. About ten feet and several toes. God, I hate that. I hate that like poison. *(extends a hand to* **NICK***)* Hello, I'm the alimony man.

NICK. *(formally)* I'm Nick…

MANNY. *(brightly)* "Good goods"!! *(to* **KIT***)* Isn't that what you mother calls him? *(to* **NICK***)* You should hear what her mother calls me!

KIT. *(seething)* Why did you come in the back?! Trying to sneak up on us?

MANNY. How'd I know you and loverboy were being kissy-wissy in front of the fire? I put my car in the garage next to yours – *(to* **NICK***)* Such a pretty picture – just like slippers under the bed.

NICK. *(looks at his watch. To* **KIT***)* Sorry, darling, but I'm late. You're sure there's no way for you to get away?

KIT. *(shakes her head)* Even if there were, you know me and parties.

MANNY. *(to KIT, going on)* I love that old VD of yours.

KIT. VW.

MANNY. *(to KIT)* What did I say?

KIT. *(stonily)* Nevermind.

MANNY. *(to NICK)* Kit used to pick me up in it. Yes, sir, whenever I was suicidal, we'd get in the back seat and she'd make my spirit rise.

KIT. *(to NICK)* Manny's the most interesting teller of dull tales I know.

MANNY. *(to KIT)* The first time we met you picked me up. And I don't mean in your Volkswagen.

KIT. *(to NICK, nervously)* He was playing with some rotten rock group in some wretched disco and…

MANNY. And you asked me if I had hair on my back.

KIT. *(to MANNY, irritated)* I seriously doubt that, but, yes, I was the first to speak. *(to NICK, lightly)* Terrified he was going to be turned down. Manny seriously can't handle rejection.

NICK. *(to MANNY)* Then I hope you won't be distressed by my saying goodbye.

MANNY. *(to NICK)* I'll walk you out.

KIT. *(to NICK)* *I'll* walk you out. *(to MANNY)* *If* you don't mind.

(**KIT** *takes* **NICK***'s arm, they turn for the front door…)*

MANNY. *(dreamily)* I just ran my hand over your seat – of your VW – feeling-it-up sorta, remembering those lip-smackin', finger-licking good ol' times! *(to NICK)* Did she pick you up, too?

NICK. Well, she's helped me manage lift-off.

KIT. "Tira Mi Su" is my middle name.

(**NICK** *turns and crosses to the front door.)*

MANNY. Nice little baubles on your ears, Kit. Who's been stuffing your stocking?

(**KIT** *fumes, turns and hurries after* **NICK**…)

KIT. We're just lucky he didn't pull down his pants and moon for us! That's one of his specialties!

NICK. You mean, show us what an asshole he is!

(**NICK** *and* **KIT** *exit, leaving the door open.* **MANNY** *rushes to the open door…*)

MANNY. *(yells) Would you like me to do that?! (starts to unbuckle his pants)* I'd be happy to… *(suddenly stops)* Son-of-a-bitch! He's giving her a…a big wet toilet plunger!!

(**MANNY** *stands back and slams the door loudly. He crosses the room, takes off his car coat, throws it on the arm of the sofa.* **KIT** *enters…*)

KIT. *(slamming front door)* Well, I must say, *that* was attractive!

MANNY. *(pleading whine)* Don't yell at me, *pleeese.*

KIT. Don't whine! And just let me tell you what I am not going to put up with this trip! Not one more minute of your goddamn stupid, fucking infantile behavior! It's Christmas for Christsake! So let's just call a truce and goddamn well try to relax and fucking enjoy it!

(silence)

MANNY. *(calmly, quietly; comic righteousness)* Kit! I've been meaning to talk to you about your language! Who've you been hanging around with?

KIT. Our son.

MANNY. *("saintly")* Well, you know how I hate scenes. How I hate confrontations.

KIT. Now I suppose you'll sulk for the duration!

MANNY. *(softly angelic)* If I've done something wrong, I'm sorry.

KIT. *(furiously)* You're always sorry after you've provoked everyone into a frenzy!

(**MANNY** *is silent, hangs his head.*)

KIT. Better not pout, Manny. *You-Know-Who's* coming to town.

(JOSH has come midway down the stairs. KIT quickly pulls off the diamond earrings before JOSH can see them and unceremoniously plops them in the fishbowl.)

JOSH. *(to MANNY)* I figured you must have arrived from the sound of the artillery down here.

(Both MANNY and KIT turn toward JOSH.)

MANNY. *(tentatively, but with great warmth)* Hi, handsome.

JOSH. *(tonelessly)* Hi.

MANNY. Do I get a kiss?

(MANNY crosses to the bottom of the stairs, holds out his arms. JOSH looks at KIT. She doesn't move or react. Finally, JOSH comes down the remainder of the stairs and kisses MANNY on the cheek and MANNY hugs him. KIT restrains a smile, looks away.)

MANNY. How've you been?

JOSH. Okay.

MANNY. How's school?

JOSH. Okay.

MANNY. You're looking great.

JOSH. So do you. How do you keep a tan in December?

MANNY. It's easy in California. There's a tanning salon on every corner.

(Feebly laughs at his joke. JOSH doesn't.)

– Do you watch the show?

JOSH. It comes on too late for a school night.

MANNY. Well, I have all of them on tape. You can see them when you come to visit. Or I can send them to you. That is, if you want me to. *(an awkward pause)* Hey, I have some presents for you. They're out in the kitchen...

(MANNY starts for the swinging door.)

JOSH. I'll open them tomorrow, with Nell.

MANNY. *(stops)* Okay. Where is my Nellie?

JOSH. Asleep. If you can believe it. *(looks at* **KIT***)* And you have the nerve to talk about *my* language.

*(***JOSH*** *turns and starts up the stairs.)*

MANNY. *(to* **JOSH***)* Goodnight.

*(***JOSH*** *doesn't answer, continues up.* **KIT** *watches him disappear, looks a bit worried.* **MANNY** *turns to her.)*

MANNY. How are they?

KIT. Ohh, Nell's a wonder.

MANNY. Yeah…and Josh? *Not* so wonderful?

*(***KIT** *has gone to the foot of the stairs to look up. She gestures silently to* **MANNY***.)*

KIT. *(quietly)* Later.

MANNY. *(nods, shrugs, changes the subject)* Well…you look nice.

KIT. *(sweetly)* Thanks. You look nice, too.

MANNY. Nice is such a nice word, isn't it?

KIT. Isn't it though. But that's how you always wanted things, right?

MANNY. Right. Just always wanted everything to be nice.

KIT. *(re: the house)* How does the house look?

MANNY. Like something out of Currier and Ives. *(thinking he may have said the wrong thing)* Only *cozier.* Warm and homey. Even…sexy.

KIT. Thanks.

MANNY. You could always make a place look cozy and warm and homey and sexy and…nice.

KIT. *(after a moment)* How's Wendy?

MANNY. Fine.

KIT. And you?

MANNY. Fine.

KIT. Fine is such a *nice* word.

MANNY. Isn't it, though. But that's how you always wanted everything. I wanted everything to be *nice* and you wanted everything to be fine. And how are *you?*

KIT. Fine – *what else?*! It's what nice people answer no matter what. People say it when they're falling apart inside – although that is not necessarily the case at the moment.

(A pause. They look at each other.)

MANNY. Wendy's pregnant. And that's not nice. And she wants to get married. And that's not fine. And I'm falling apart inside.

KIT. *(seriously)* I'm sorry you're not happy, Manny.

MANNY. Oh, I'm happy! I didn't say I wasn't happy. I said I was...

KIT. I heard you. What are you and Wendy going to do?

MANNY. Well, I don't want to get married and she doesn't want an abortion so, I don't know – a double suicide, I suppose.

*(**KIT** is silent.)*

MANNY. *(after a moment)* But everything's gonna be just fine. Life's good. I like myself – most of the time. I like Wendy, most of the time – like my house, like my Mercedes.

KIT. A Mercedes...well. I hear there're as common as avocadoes out there.

*(**MANNY** lets that pass. **KIT** goes to the sofa, sits down.)*

MANNY. Bernie's blossomed, really. Got color. Gets exercise. Gone Hollywood.

KIT. And the lady with the hat?

MANNY. The lady with the hat is a different story. As you know, Mable never wanted to move out there in the first place. She *loves* the city. Loves the streets, adores the filth, craves the noise, can't get enough of the violence.

KIT. I like your mother so much more than I like mine.

MANNY. All she ever wanted was to live in a building with a doorman on Park Avenue. That's all I've heard ever since I was a kid in Brooklyn. Well, a building with a doorman she got.

KIT. She wrote me you bought them a condominium.

MANNY. Yeah, and it has a pimply-faced kid with a funny hat who *sometimes* opens the door. But it's not on Park Avenue in Manhattan – it's on Ocean Avenue in Santa Monica. And Mabel doesn't give a fuck-all for the climate or the cleanliness or the security of it all! She's starved for some pissing freezing cold muggins, some sky-high garbage, a few blistering insults. The lady in the hat wants *action*! They both make me nuts!

(KIT laughs. MANNY moves to the sofa.)

MANNY. How's Corinne?

KIT. Still making *me* nuts. Still complaining. Always about the heaviest of issues like…they've stopped making satin lingerie cases in her color of champagne beige.

MANNY. Your mother is sort of champagne beige head to toe. Her hair, her skin, her clothes. In fact, Corinne is sort of a champagne beige name.

KIT. No wonder my father was an alcoholic.

MANNY. Do you suppose our kids are going to feel the same about us? Love us. Hate us.

KIT. They already do.

MANNY. *(mild panic attack)* Oh, god, oh, god, I'm going to faint!

KIT. *(not indulging him)* No you're not. Take a deep breath and you'll be fine.

MANNY. Oh my god, I left my blood-pressure machine in the car!

KIT. Do you still have that stupid thing?

(Slight pause as MANNY inhales, exhales deeply, then sits down beside her, resting his head on the back of the sofa, feeling his pulse.)

(after a moment) Why is it that you still go out of your way to insult anyone in whom I have the least bit of interest?

MANNY. *(sits up)* Oh, well, you can't be serious about *him*! He looks like he's been delivering balloons all his life!

KIT. When you used to do it on the road, I'd flatter myself that you were being the jealous husband – though why I was ever fool enough to make you breakfast when you stumbled in after fucking some little groupie all night, I'll never know.

MANNY. *(mock sweetly, almost batting his eyes)* I always came home though, didn't I? Didn't I, *darling*?

KIT. You did it when you were here this summer – with that fellow on the Yale faculty I was seeing.

MANNY. Oh, well, he was a joke! I mean, do you know he actually said to me that rock and roll was *declasse*?! God, am I glad you dumped *him*!

KIT. *(laughs)* You know what? I am, too.

MANNY. *(laughing at himself)* Declasse, that's me. Can you believe this rock and roll schmuck is now an honest-to-god Hollywood composer?

KIT. I knew you'd make it. *(sweetly)* I hope you get everything you want, Manny. I want you to be happy.

(He smiles warmly at her, brushes her chin with his fingertip. She takes his hand – at first it is to discourage his being too intimate…then, she looks at his hand thoughtfully, holds on to it a second before letting it go.)

You always had the most beautiful hands – graceful as a dancer's. I always loved the curve in your wrists, the way your long, slender fingers stay together, cupped ever so slightly – like the head of a swan. Music just has to come out of them.

*(Sight pause…***MANNY** *is entranced.)*

MANNY. *(hushed)* What can I tell you, Kit, I'm jealous. When I see you with someone else I just hate it like poison.

*(***KIT** *looks into* **MANNY***'s eyes.)*

KIT. You've done well for yourself, Manny. Maybe the divorce brought you luck.

MANNY. *(horrified)* Oh, Kit, don't say that!

> *(A pause as they continue to look at each other. Finally, she gets up, moves away. He tries to break the mood, too, gets up and heads for the swinging door.)*

> *(en route)* There are presents from my folks, too – for the kids and for you. And some things from me, of course.

> *(He exits to the kitchen. She goes over to the fireplace, and with the poker fishes out an unburned cigarette, puts it in her lips, lets it rest there a moment, then jerks it out and hurls it back in the fire.)*

KIT. *(loud enough for* **MANNY** *to hear)* I hope they didn't buy me clothes. They always buy me things I have to take back – and then I always feel so guilty and unappreciative.

> *(***MANNY*** *re-enters with an armful of wrapped presents and his garment bag.* **KIT** *goes to help him.)*

MANNY. Here, this one's for you from them.

> *(He hands her a large hexagonal box.)*

KIT. *(anxiously)* Oh, god, you don't suppose it's a hat, do you? This looks like it could be a hatbox.

MANNY. *(dismissively)* Oh, they've learned their lesson. They said they've never seen you wear a thing they've given you so this year they were getting you something very "blah." Mabel's exact word.

KIT. What's blah that could come in a hexagon box? Oh, I just know it's a hat. An *eight-sided* hat!

> *(***MANNY*** *has hung his garment bag on the newell post, taken the other presents over to the tree...)*

MANNY. Listen, they know how hard you are to please.

KIT. *(incredulously)* Hard to please?

MANNY. *(quickly)* I mean, how *precise* you are. How you like things your way.

KIT. *(glares)* My way?

MANNY. You know what I mean – "just so."

KIT. We just have very different taste, that's all!

MANNY. Yes, that's true – but you must admit, you can be very rigid.

KIT. *(tightly)* Yes, I admit I *can* be. *Could* be. I'm different than I used to be!

MANNY. Good! How?

KIT. I'm actually trying. Can't you see how there're coffee stains on the slipcovers? And I never run around fluffing up the down cushions every time they're sat on.

MANNY. Well, congratulations.

KIT. I'm not quite out of the woods yet, but I'm working on it. Actually, it's my New Year's resolution: to be more flexible – less rigid about everything.

MANNY. Great! God, how I hated it when you'd get a case of the "perfects."

KIT. The "perfects?"

MANNY. Just like your mother.

KIT. What a thoroughly shitty thing to say to me!

MANNY. And when the holidays rolled around it really would be nuclear family launchpad!

KIT. You hated the holidays long before you ever met me!

MANNY. Right. I'd like to mow down shoppers! I'd like to slaughter reindeer! I'd like to detonate the North Pole!

KIT. Well, I happen to love the holidays! *All* of them! I always have!

MANNY. Yeah, who needs a calendar with you around – homemade Valentines, satin hearts and paper lace. And pretty soon it's Easter baskets and Easter bunnies and bunnysuits and dyed eggs and dyed chicks and dead ducks and chocolate-covered everything but chocolate-covered crucifixes!

KIT. *(defensively)* I just love getting in the spirit of things! I see nothing wrong with that!

MANNY. *(hardly drawing breath)* And bammo! Before you know it, it's homebaked birthday cakes with special sayings and party hats and pin-the-tail on the donkey, and lookout, folks! It's fireworks for the fourth of July, bakeoffs and cookouts and hoop-dee-do and *hello*, it's Halloween! Pumpkins stabbed into jack-o-lanterns and funny faces and trick or treat, and before-you-know-it, *tahdahmm*! it's a turkey for Thanksgiving, and a *goose* for Christmas and *whoops*, thank-you-very-much!

KIT. Cynical bastard!

MANNY. *(really rolling)* ...And Ho, ho, ho, it's Christmas cards and a Christmas tree, hand-picked and hand-hewn, and wreathes and garlands and boughs and bows on boxes stacked to the ceiling! And enough food for a famine, and none of that sto' bought business for you, oh, no, your little oven's sayin' lovin' morning, noon, and night with pies and puds and nogs and grogs, and gimme a break! – and god-almighty when and where does it ever for fuckin' sake end??!!

(a pause)

KIT. So I overdid it.

MANNY. And you wonder why I tried to pretend the holidays didn't exist – tried to look the other way?!

KIT. *(flaring)* Okay! Overdone! Overdecorated! Over-the-top! I wanted a home.

MANNY. Oh, was that it?!

KIT. It's all I ever wanted! All my life! A real home with a real family – a family that looks at each other and speaks to each other and *screams* at each other! One that doesn't just take each other for granted and shut each other out. One that's *alive*! Not like the dead thing I grew up with. Not like what I had with you: nobody at home, nobody ever in! *(pause; calmly)* What's your New Year's resolution?

MANNY. *(calmly)* Ohh, I don't know, I haven't thought about it. Let's see...try to thaw the Wall-Of-Silence, I guess.

KIT. *(applauds)* Congratulations to you, too!

MANNY. Well, I'm still working on it. Not quite there yet, either. But I'm *trying* to communicate. Trying not to shy away from confrontations, trying not to tune out, tune off…

KIT. The trouble is that you think saying what's on your mind is always a confrontation. You think talking to each other has to turn into a war. All I ever wanted was a simple exchange of thoughts and word – so that some molehill wouldn't turn into some Mont Blanc which you could misunderstand and sulk about!

MANNY. *(after a moment)* Well, with a little luck, maybe we'll both come through. Change is possible. Growth is possible. I believe that.

(Pause. He stares at her. She looks away.)

(simply) It's good to see you.

KIT. *(looks directly at him)* It's good to see you, too. *(slight, awkward pause, then)* Let me help you put your things upstairs. In your room.

(She goes to take the garment bag. He picks up the duffel bag and joins her at the stairs.)

MANNY. You know Mabel and Bernie tell me everytime they speak to you.

KIT. That reminds me, I owe them a call. Oh, god, how I despise Alexander Graham Bell.

MANNY. Every time you call *them*, they call *me*.

KIT. Well, I do try to make an effort on birthdays…and special occasions. I want the kids to know their grandparents.

(KIT has turned and started up the stairs but MANNY's next speech stops her midway.)

MANNY. My mother said you told her, "Just because Manny and I are divorced, it doesn't mean *we* can't be friends." – That meant a lot to them. They love you, you know.

KIT. And I love them.

MANNY. I hope we can be friends, too.

KIT. *(sincerely)* We are friends, Manny. We always have been. Let's just try to be better ones. For everybody's sake.

MANNY. *(sincerely)* It's a deal. Shake it like you mean it?

*(He hold out a hand. She holds out her hand. But **MANNY** doesn't take it. Rather, after a beat, he sticks out his rear end and shakes it.)*

*(**KIT** doesn't react, just silently stares at him and lowers her hand. **MANNY** stops, realizes his joke has fallen flat.)*

(apologetic plea) Sorry! I'm going to try to stop acting like a clown, too! Honest, I am – but, oh, Kit, I just hate being so goddamn solemn about it. I hate it like "pois-*son*" – French for poison.

KIT. *(coolly)* "Pois*son*" is French for fish.

MANNY. Well, pardonez-moi for living.

*(A moment, then **KIT** silently extends her hand again. He leaps upon it, shaking her hand vigorously and gratefully.)*

(ecstatically) Christ, this new year's not going to be *long* enough or *wide* enough or *tall* enough to contain our mental health!

*(**KIT** laughs, turns and goes upstairs and **MANNY** follows.)*

*(The stage is empty for a moment. Then, the swinging door is slowly pushed open and **JOSH** comes into the room. He looks toward the stairs, then turns to see **MANNY**'s coat lying on the arm of the sofa. He slowly crosses to it, picks it up and tries it on.)*

*(**JOSH** walks about, getting the feel of the coast, obviously not disliking it. He spots the presents **MANNY** has brought which were put under the tree. He crosses to pick them up and look at the cards until he finds the one that's meant for him. He holds it a moment, shakes it, and then puts it back.)*

*(Now **JOSH** reaches for the switch and turns the tree on and it illuminates with a spirited glow.)*

(There is an offstage sound – voices and footsteps at the top of the stairs. **JOSH** *snaps his head in that direction, quickly jumps up and takes off the coat and puts it back where it was, then runs out the swinging door.)*

(Momentarily, **MANNY** *comes down the stairs, pausing in the center of the room, sensing that someone has just been there. He looks to see that the tree is lit as* **KIT** *comes downstairs.)*

MANNY. *(cont.)* Is it my imagination or was the tree not lit when we went upstairs?

KIT. *(not getting the question)* Ohh, it looks lovely! Did you turn it on?

MANNY. I didn't touch it.

KIT. Who, then? Some little elf?

MANNY. Yeah, some little fifteen year-old elf.

KIT. *(comprehending)* Ohh. Want a drink?

MANNY. Got any club soda?

KIT. No egg nog? Or fruit cake?

MANNY. Fruit cake?!

KIT. Forget I said that.

(She goes to the bar, opens a bottle of soda and puts it over ice.)

MANNY. *(re: playing Santa)* So where do we begin?

KIT. The closet. Behind the coats and ladder and stuff…

*(***MANNY** *goes to the closet door under the stairs, opens it, removes the stepladder, pushes coats aside, removes several pieces of luggage to reveal an old steamer trunk, plastered with hotel stickers.)*

MANNY. *(pulling out the trunk)* Oh, you've still got this great old trunk of your dad's.

KIT. *(crosses to hand him the soda)* The toys are inside.

*(***MANNY** *takes the soda, drinks, sets it down. He opens the trunk to reveal some toys – some in boxes, some unwrapped.* **KIT** *starts to place some of them around the room.* **MANNY** *does likewise.)*

KIT. How's your friend? And I don't mean Wendy.

MANNY. Who?

KIT. The violin player. Colin – ?

MANNY. Oh! Well, now, Colin is probably the first close friend I've had in my life. I mean, other than you. He's fine now. What's this?

(He holds a long, narrow, soft carrying case made of a synthetic material.)

KIT. *(looks up)* Josh's BB gun. And his friend died?

MANNY. *(shakes his head)* Yeah. AIDS. Terrible. He was *my* age! I never really thought of anyone *my age* dying. His death really shook me up.

KIT. *(sardonically)* Not to mention what it must have done to Colin.

MANNY. Oh, he was a mess. I must say – and I say this in all modesty – if it hadn't been for me, I think he would have cracked up.

KIT. I'm glad you were there for him.

MANNY. Yeah, I'm a much more generous person than I used to be.

KIT. I'm glad to hear that.

MANNY. How's your sister?

KIT. She got married again. To the same guy.

MANNY. The Frog?

KIT. *(nods)* The rich, powerful, socially correct Frog.

MANNY. I wonder what it is that draws two people back together again and makes them get married all over.

KIT. *(looks at him directly)* Masochism. Sadomasochism.

*(**MANNY** gives her a look, wheels out a miniature baby carriage, then removes a kite-shaped object in a felt cloth bag, gathered with a drawstring at one end. He unties the sack to peer inside.)*

MANNY. What's this wicked looking thing? *(He starts to remove it from the sack…)*

KIT. *(looks over)* Josh's crossbow.

(**MANNY** *takes out a modern steel version of the medieval variety…*)

MANNY. Hmmmmm. *(hangs the crossbow on the armoire door)* You know, I knew. I knew from the first time I saw you.

KIT. Knew what?

MANNY. From the first moment I laid eyes on you, I knew we were gonna get in some trouble together. And I think you knew it, too.

KIT. I did. And I think that about says it: "get in some trouble together." Why not, "support, extend, enrich each other?" Rather than cause each other some trouble.

MANNY. I don't know. I wonder what it is? There was this tremendous physical attraction, of course, but there was something behind your eyes, something that let me know…*here's the one.*

KIT. *(stops, says softly)* Yes, Manny, I saw something behind your eyes, too.

(They look at each other for a moment. She turns away, begins to gather up some wrapping and put it into a cardboard box.)

*(**MANNY** has removed a baby doll and two other items. He holds one up to **KIT**…)*

MANNY. This, I take it, is Josh's hunting knife.

*(**MANNY** puts the doll under his arm and pulls the knife from its scabbard, flashing the blade…)*

KIT. That's right.

MANNY. And this?

*(**MANNY** brandishes the second item.)*

KIT. …is his foil for his fencing lessons.

MANNY. You don't think it means anything, do you, that he only requested weapons for Christmas?

KIT. Listen, I drew the line at the Do-it-Yourself W.M.D. Kit.

(She pulls out a baseball bat, hands it to him.)

– Here. Add this to the arsenal.

MANNY. I'm serious!

KIT. I'm so glad you are. Because it *is* serious.

MANNY. What is? What is going on?

(**KIT** *has moves to the stairs, looks up.*)

KIT. *(looks back to* **MANNY,** *softly)* Later.

MANNY. *(picks up her hushed tone)* You keep saying, "Later. Later." Why not *now, now*?

KIT. *(hushed)* He's still up. I can hear him. And he can hear us.

(**MANNY** *sighs, nods, goes to get a particular present he has brought – something that looks like a dress box from an expensive store.*)

MANNY. This is for you from me.

KIT. Shouldn't I wait for the kids?

MANNY. *(shakes his head)* Uh-uh.

KIT. *(takes the package, looks at label)* Oh, my, Rodeo Drive, Beverly Hills, no less!

MANNY. No smart, East Coast cracks, please.

(*She opens the box to remove an expensive, hand-made black satin bra and pair of black satin panties, trimmed with sheer black lace.*)

KIT. Oh, my, they're…they're lovely.

MANNY. The lace – blind nuns or something.

KIT. At the very least. Thank you. They're…well, they're *stunning*. I'm truly…*stunned*.

MANNY. You really mean it? You don't hate them?

KIT. I really mean it, Manny – and I don't mean to sound ungrateful, but do you think they're appropriate?

MANNY. Appropriate? You mean, for the climate? I figured you had enough longjohns.

KIT. I mean isn't it the sort of thing you ought to give to Wendy rather than me?

MANNY. I only know it's probably something I wouldn't have given you when we were married. *(thinks; after a moment)* Maybe I've learned something from Wendy.

KIT. Yes, maybe you have. *(puts the lingerie back in the box)* I hope you don't mind, but I think I'm actually more interested in hearing about Colin than I am about Wendy.

MANNY. Oh. Okay. He's, well…he's a terrific musician. He and his fiddle are very much in demand. I always use him on the recording dates for the show. He does "avec schmaltz" great.

KIT. Avec what?

MANNY. Schmaltz. The lovey-dovey string stuff. That's how all those European composers who wound up in Hollywood used to mark the romantic passages in their scores. Especially the violin solos. Colin's fingers are more sentimental than Mother's Day.

KIT. Can we leave mothers out of this?

MANNY. *(shrugs)* I love Colin. We have lunch at the studio and play tennis sometime and schmooze about our careers and, of course, the life and times of Manny Boy.

KIT. *(dryly)* Mmmm. Well, who else?!

MANNY. You'd like him. You have a lot in common. You could talk about music and books and old movies… and you could talk about me.

KIT. You're so endlessly fascinating, I can't see how we'd have much time to cover anything else.

MANNY. You two have the same sort of sensitivity toward "*The Rules.*"

KIT. What rules would those be?

MANNY. You know, *The Unwritten Rules.* He would never come over without calling first. He would never cancel at the last minute, and if he were going to be late, he'd call to say he was going to be late. And he always calls the next day to say, thank you – or worse, writes a note. And he never forgets holidays, birthdays or anniversaries. He's just brimming over with all them there decent, humane, civilized qualities I never heard of.

KIT. Are you making fun of me?

MANNY. Would I do such a thing?

KIT. *Would* and *have* and *are*. I think.

MANNY. Don't be ridiculous. If anything, I'm lamenting my own shortcomings.

KIT. Well, maybe there's hope for you yet. You used to not know you *had* any shortcomings. Just keep hanging around Colin. I approve.

MANNY. Yeah, what happened to "Goodtime Manny," our irresponsible, emotionally adolescent friend – sex and drugs and rock and rollin' down the runway of life! I'm so sedentary now Wendy and I are almost like an old married couple. Different from the way *we* were a married couple. Different priorities. Different arrangement. Different sexually.

KIT. This is where I came in. I take it you're referring to what you've learned from Wendy. Well, okay, what is it? Can you *say*? Will you say?

(She crosses with a basket of goodies: candy canes, nuts, trinkets, etc. She starts to fill the stockings.)

MANNY. So you *are* interested. You're sure you really want to know?

KIT. You know goddamn well I want to know! I'm a big girl, Manny. I can take it.

MANNY. *(sip of his soda)* Well…it's not that she's better than you – or that it's better with her than it was with you – or that it was lousy with *us*…

KIT. *(stops, turns to him) Sometimes* it was lousy! And then, again, sometimes it was great.

MANNY. Yeah, when it was good it was great. For me, anyway.

KIT. When it was great it was good for me, too.

(She turns back to the business of the stockings.)

MANNY. With Wendy, it's just *different*, that's all. She's more…well, *I'm* more…well…

KIT. What?

MANNY. Free-er. There's something with her that allows me to be less inhibited. To be…well, for lack of a better word: *wilder*. I do things with her I never dreamt of doing with you.

KIT. *(tolerantly, her back still to him)* I never knew you were inhibited with me. That I inhibited you.

MANNY. I know you never meant to.

KIT. *(wheels around)* Never *meant* to! I had no idea that's how you perceived me!

MANNY. *(staying cool – or trying to)* I'm saying that it was coming from me, not from you. Anyway, that's how it was.

*(**KIT** throws the basket into the overstuffed chair, steps forward to confront him.)*

KIT. Well, you certainly were a pretty good actor, that's all I can say! You certainly gave one helluva fine performance!

MANNY. I wasn't performing *all the time.*

KIT. *(boiling)* Just *some* of the time.

MANNY. I really meant it *most* of the time. And *always* up to a certain point.

KIT. What *point*, may I inquire, was that?!

MANNY. I think it's because I don't love Wendy that I can have more fun in bed with her. There don't seem to be any terrible consequences involved.

KIT. *(incredulous)* What terrible consequences?! What are you talking about?!

MANNY. I knew you weren't going to take this well.

KIT. *(sardonically) Did* you?! I wonder why?!

MANNY. I think we ought to just drop it. I don't want to talk about it anymore.

KIT. *(quickly)* Oh, no you don't! You're not going to pull that with me now!

MANNY. You know how I hate…

KIT. *Communication!*

MANNY. *(softly)* I just want everything nice!

KIT. *(bluntly)* Is this the old wife vs. mistress story? You can't enjoy fucking your wife because she's your mother and she's on a pedestal?! But you can really get-it-off with some bimbo?!

MANNY. Wendy's not a bimbo! She's an executive!

KIT. I don't care what she is, I know the type – her hair is longer than her skirt!

MANNY. Bimbo!

KIT. This girl sounds very talented.

MANNY. *(grinning)* Ohh, she's *verr-y* talented.

KIT. You like it better with her than with me!

MANNY. I didn't say that. I said it was *different!*

KIT. What?! Toys?! Donkeys?! Chandeliers?! *What?!*

MANNY. That's not what I'm talking about and you know it!

KIT. I don't know *what* you're talking about! Why don't you just say what you're talking and then I'll know. You always expect me to be some kind of a goddamn mind reader. I guess I was expected to be clairvoyant in bed.

MANNY. *(slightly pouty)* That's not what I'm talking about at all.

KIT. *(an exhausted plea)* Speak, Manny! Tell me what you're talking about! *(quieter)* You said I was your friend. Well, I was and I am. I still am. For god's sake for once, open up and say what's on your mind.

(Pause. **MANNY** *sits in the overstuffed chair.)*

MANNY. *(quietly, evenly)* I'm not afraid to let go with her. With you I always felt like I had to stay in control. The more you enjoyed it, the more you let yourself go, the more you got into it, the more anxious I'd get. The more I'd get scared. Terrified. Petrified. With her I can let myself go and get lost in it and enjoy it and not be afraid. I only wish I could do that with someone I love.

(Pause. **KIT** *sits on the arm of the chair beside him.)*

KIT. *(sincerely)* Thanks for telling me. I mean that. Thank you for, at last, letting me in on exactly what's going on in your head. It helps. It really helps. *(silence from* **MANNY***)* Do you have any idea what you were terrified of? What the consequences really are? *(silence from* **MANNY***)* Manny…*please…*

MANNY. *(after a long moment)* I just know that the way you loved me scared the shit out of me. And I felt that if I went with it, that I'd fall apart – that I might even go crazy. That I might not get back. That I might die.

KIT. How very sad.

MANNY. I guess making contact with someone I love is something so unknown to me that it quite simply frightens me to death.

KIT. *(going easy)* And why shouldn't it? You don't have much practice with people unless they're right on top of you or three feet away.

(Pause. **MANNY** *puts his hands over his face.* **KIT** *puts her arm around him.)*

MANNY. Yeah… Either Bernie all over me like some infestation of locusts or Mabel never quite within reach. Sat by me and taught me to play the piano. But always from a distance…well, about…

KIT. Three feet.

MANNY. *(nods)* And I'd chase her and grab her, but it didn't work. She didn't exactly pull away or push me away… she'd just *melt* away. Evaporate. Her laugh would die, her smile would fade and she'd…remove…herself just about three feet in distance.

KIT. *(almost to herself)* No happy medium. Never. For either one of us. No…*reality.*

(A moment and **MANNY** *straightens up and* **KIT** *removes her arm. He takes the last swallow of his soda, gets up, goes to the armoire, empties the remainder of the bottle into his glass.)*

MANNY. Colin's all for our getting back together again.

*(**KIT** doesn't respond, gets up, picks up the basket, resumes stuffing the stockings.)*

MANNY. He thinks you're wonderful. He knows everything about you. Everything. The works.

KIT. How odd – having someone you never laid eyes on know how you are in bed.

*(**MANNY** crosses to her.)*

MANNY. Oh, Kit, I've made such a mess of things! I've really come here this time to tell you that!

(She stops, puts down the basket, crosses to the tree, adjusts some ornaments.)

(urgently) I realized it when I was here this summer. And when I got back to California and told Colin how I felt, it all came clear. I know what a fuck-up I am. What an impossible son-of-a-bitch I've been, but I've changed…I'm *trying* to change. Can't we…can't *we* give it another try?

KIT. *(goes to bay window, looks out; simply)* You'd leave me again. I just know it. If you don't actually leave town, you mentally check out. What do you think it's like living with a goddamn zombie?

MANNY. No laughs, to say the least.

KIT. You got it. No laughs *at all.* When Josh was six years old, do you remember what he said? "Who is that man who lives with us?"

MANNY. You think that didn't get to me?

KIT. You'd hole-up in a room for days on end and when you'd finally emerge, you'd come into the kitchen and never speak to us, never say one word – just devour a box of jelly doughnuts, standing over the sink, then go back and close the door again. "Who is that man who lives with us?" It was a good question. And one to which I did not have the answer.

MANNY. I didn't know who I was myself.

KIT. You weren't there when Josh was born. I told people you were on the road, but you were…where *were* you?

MANNY. Just sitting in our apartment in shock. Twenty years old and a *father*!

KIT. It happens.

MANNY. Not to me. Not to Manny – loverboy, lunatic, life-of-the-party! I didn't even want to get married, so who wanted a kid?!

KIT. I wanted a kid.

MANNY. I wanted you to get rid of it.

KIT. I wanted to get married.

MANNY. I wanted to run. I remember Bernie came to find me – said everyone had been looking high and low and lo and behold! – where was I? In bed with my clothes on under the covers, staring at the ceiling. *(crosses to the fireplace, hyperventilating)* Jesus, is it hot in here?!

KIT. *(sardonically)* Not for us grownups.

(He turns, gives her a look, crosses back to pick up his glass and return to the armoire to fill it with ice cubes.)

*(**KIT** crosses to the fireplace, takes the poker, adjusts the fire.)*

MANNY. You know what, Kit? I can see me in Josh and it makes me want to kill myself. God, I don't want him to be like me. I wouldn't wish that on…on Nick, let alone my own kid!

KIT. *(turns to him, calmly)* I'm worried about Josh, Manny. He's so smart and so sensitive. Sensitive as a leaf and just about as sturdy in a windstorm. He's so hurt. And *sooo* angry. Some part of him feels deeply responsible for our breaking up. I'm afraid he's going to do something senseless to somebody – or to himself.

MANNY. *(puts down his glass)* What exactly is going on? What happened?

KIT. Two weeks ago Friday, he asked me if he could spend the night at his friend's, a really good kid I like – even though he's a bit older, he's about the only one I'm not totally terrified about Josh being around. Three-thirty Saturday morning, the police arrived at the door…

MANNY. Police?! Shit! What?!

KIT. He had totaled his friend's car. The other boy has a fractured pelvis and is still in the hospital. Josh wasn't hurt – just shook up and in shock. There're weren't any drugs or alcohol involved, but anyway, Manny – he's dancing near the flame.

MANNY. *(anxiously)* Oh, Jesus, Josh and Nellie – when I think of where I've failed them and how their little minds are turning and twisting, my pulse plays the Minute Waltz in thirty-seven seconds!

KIT. Will you take him aside tomorrow – talk to him and try to get him to talk to you? I know it's not your style, but…

MANNY. My style! My style sucks! *(sighs)* Sure. I'll give it my best shot. God knows, I love him and I'm glad he's ours. You do believe that, don't you?

KIT. Of course, I do.

MANNY. *(after a moment)* You know, it's lucky for some we married each other. Instead of four people being unhappy, only two were. *(looks at her very directly)* I know it's not enough to say I'm sorry. But I am. Couldn't we…?

KIT. *(tearing, stops him)* No, Manny, no. I could never take your silences again. I could never allow you to freeze me out anymore. Ever again.

(He pulls a silk scarf from his jacket pocket, hands it to her. She dries her tears.)

MANNY. Oh, Kit, I love your eyes-they're so…so…

KIT. …so red and green?

MANNY. Kit, I know it sounds crazy but…come to California with me!

KIT. *(moving away from him)* What??

MANNY. *(following)* For New Year's! We'll do Christmas here together, but then let's leave! Together! All of us! Kids and all, Kit and kaboodle!

KIT. Manny, I just happen to be practically engaged to another guy.

MANNY. Oh, you don't care about *him*! Not *that* way! I know you don't. Say yes! Say you will! Say you'll come and celebrate with me – caviar and champagne, corks popping like cannon fire!

KIT. This doesn't sound like you, Manny. You were never a virtuoso with romantic underscoring.

MANNY. It's the new me! Ring out the old, ring in the bright, shiny new – filled with promise and hope, resolves and resolutions. Ring, ring, ring!

(The doorbell rings…)

KIT. Who could that be?

MANNY. *(furious)* I don't know, but if it's Santa Claus his timing is shit!

*(**KIT** runs to the front door…)*

KIT. *(crossing)* I hope it's not the police! I hope Josh didn't sneak out the back and bludgeon someone.

*(She tears the door open to reveal…Santa Claus! or someone in a red suit and a white beard [**MANNY**].)*

MANNY. *(crossing)* I was just saying what lousy timing you have!!

KIT. *(rattled)* NICK!! – What are you *doing* here?!

*(**NICK** steps inside, **KIT** closes the door.)*

NICK. *(excitedly)* Forgive me, Kit, but I just know he's come here to pull something funny and I had to come back!

MANNY. GET OUT! GET OUT!

NICK. You're too important to me to risk…

MANNY. OUT-OUT!

NICK. I love you, Kit, and I want you to marry me! *(takes a plush box from his pocket)* This *is* what it looks like! A plush box with a ring in it! *(notices her bare ears)* Where are the earrings I gave you?

KIT. Uh…in the fishbowl.

NICK. The fishbowl?!

*(**MANNY** has gone to grab **JOSH**'s BB gun, points it at **NICK**…)*

MANNY. Get out or I'm gonna shoot you!!

KIT. *Manny, put that down!*

NICK. OH-MY-GOD, KIT, IS THAT LOADED?!

MANNY. You better believe it's loaded!

KIT. *(to* **NICK***)* Don't worry, darling, it's only a BB gun.

NICK. So what! It could still put a hole in me!

*(**MANNY** takes aim, jumps to a crouched position.)*

MANNY. *(warrior-like)* Ah-ha!

KIT. *Manny!!*

(Suddenly, **NICK** *grabs the crossbow…)*

NICK. *AH-HA!*

KIT. *(alarmed)* NICK!!

MANNY. *(jumps back)* HEY! ARE YOU CRAZY!

(pulling the trigger over and over, but nothing happens)
– THIS FUCKING THING *ISN'T* LOADED!

NICK. *(raises the crossbow)* BUT *THIS* FUCKING THING IS!

MANNY. OH-MY-GOD, KIT, *DO SOMETHING!*

KIT. NICK! MANNY!

*(**MANNY** starts to run around the room,* **NICK** *in pursuit.* **KIT** *suddenly picks up the baseball bat, waits for them to pass, swings to hit* **NICK***. He steps out of the way and she clips* **MANNY***!)*

MANNY. AAAAOOOOOOOWWWWW!!!

KIT. *(cringes)* Ooooouuuuuuuuuuu!!!

(**MANNY** *grabs his head, drops the BB gun, stumbles about like a stunned drunk.* **KIT** *gasps.* **MANNY** *picks up the fencing foil,* **NICK** *raises the crossbow to aim at* **MANNY** *and* **KIT** *conks* **NICK** *on the head.* **NICK** *stumbles about, his beard and hat falling off.*)

(*Simultaneously,* **NELLIE** *runs down the stairs, followed by* **JOSH** *who is now also dressed in pajamas.*)

NELLIE. DADDY! DADDY! ARE YOU ALL RIGHT?!

(**MANNY** *has wobbled and fallen to the floor in front of the tree as* **NELLIE** *reaches him…*)

MANNY. *(ga-ga)* Hello, my angel…

(**NICK** *has wobbled and fallen onto the sofa and* **KIT** *has gone to him…*)

KIT. Ohh, Nick, I'm *sooo* sorry!

MANNY. *(gives her a look)* You're telling *him* you're sorry!

(**JOSH** *covers his mouth with his hands, stiffling a laugh.* **NELLIE** *has grabbed* **MANNY** *about the neck, gives him a bear hug and a big kiss and starts to sing to him…*)

NELLIE. *(bellowing)* "SI-E-LENT NIGHGHT!! HOL-LI-EEE NIGHT!!! ALL IS CALM!!!…"

(*curtain*)

ACT II

Scene One

(The living room of a nineteen-thirties Beverly Hills "hacienda." The architecture is Hollywood Hispanic – the ambience California casual. Everything is stucco, tile and wrought iron. And everything has been re-done by an expensive decorator in what might be called the "Santa Fe" school.)

(The entrance is in the center right wall, an iron-hinged, heavy wood-paneled door with a semi-circular top. There is a smaller replica if the door at eye-level: the peephole.)

(Downstage of the entrance in the left wall is a built-in contemporary bar with lighted shelves, stocked with handsome crystal bar ware. [We can't see behind the bar, but it would have a stainless sink, a fridge and ice machine.])

(Just right of the entrance is a semi-circle arch which leads to the dining room and kitchen. Just right of the arch is a curved staircase which fans up to the bedrooms off. Beneath the stairs is an arched niche, not for religious statuary, but for a telephone.)

(Up center left there is a larger semicircle arch, framing window-doors which open onto a blossoming patio, drenched in late-afternoon sunlight. [This is the route to the pool and garage, off right.])

(In the right wall is a third [smaller] arch which frames a fireplace.)

(All the furniture is up-to-the-minute. Everything is upholstered and painted in pale pastel desert shades: a sofa with end tables and a coffee table. Two comfortable

chairs at either side with tables and lamps. A highest-tech possible TV and CD components are stacked on a space-age stand down extreme left. Here and there are gigantic ceramic planters containing enormous cacti.)

(Lastly, there is a small shocking pink artificial Christmas tree, sparsely decorated with a few shocking pink balls, standing alone, forlorn in the middle of the coffee table. Like the tree, the entire place is coordinated, detached, impersonal – another kind of shop window.)

*(**A WORD TO THE SCENIC DESIGNER:** This may appear to be a complicated and expensive production with seven characters and two specific sets. Well, the play's always going to have seven characters so there's not much to be done about that but, I have devised a way for both the sets to be constructed on one turn table [even a manual one, which could be wound by-hand between the acts.] The colonial stairs in the "traditional" set lead up to an alcove behind which [on the other side of the scenery], flows the "mediterranean" cascade of steps. The side walls are on wheels and reversible: The right wall and door of the colonial house, flips and becomes the hinged-panel door entrance of the left wall. The left stone colonial fireplace, surrounded by books in shelves, flips and becomes the solid center mediterranean wall and a "plug" is struck [where the stone fireplace would be] for the indicated center left patio doors in the California house. The design for this show should be considered to be practical, economic, and clever, as opposed to a drawback.)*

*(At the top of Act II, the pastel, postmodern "mediterranean" room is empty. Presently, the front door is flung open and **NELLIE** races in, carrying her small suitcase. She's followed by **JOSH**, carrying his duffel bag as well as his sister's larger pieces of luggage. Both **JOSH** and **NELLIE** drop their things, awestruck by the place...)*

NELLIE. *Ai, caramba!* Looks sorta like that restaurant on 46th Street where we get the enchilladas when we go to a matinee.

JOSH. El Cayote Loco?

NELLIE. *(looks around)* Yeah, El Cayote Loco's – but with a better bar.

JOSH. Yeah, only this doesn't look quite as authentic.

(MANNY *has dashed inside carrying* KIT*'s suitcase and his duffel bag, both of which he drops, catching his breath. He has heard* JOSH*'s last line...)*

MANNY. Not authentic as *what*?!

JOSH. This Mexican joint in Hell's Kitchen.

MANNY. What do you mean, this is the *real thing*! The border's only about a block from here!

(JOSH *hands* MANNY *the house keys and* MANNY *rushes back outside.* NELLIE *has gone to look at the little shocking pink Christmas tree on the coffee table.* JOSH *comes over to her...)*

JOSH. Rather pitiful looking isn't it?

NELLIE. It's so pink and...pink. And the wrong pink, at that.

JOSH. Well, let's not say anything.

(NELLIE *nods and turns to start up the stairs.* JOSH *turns and begins to follow when* MANNY *dashes back in, carrying another one of* KIT*'s bags as well as his own.)*

MANNY. *(stopping them)* Oh, you two aren't up there! Mommie is going to be up there!

NELLIE. *(innocently)* In Wendy's room?

MANNY. *(tolerantly)* In the *guest* room.

JOSH. *(to* NELLIE*)* What do you mean, in Wendy's room! They sleep together. You know that. Why play dumb?

NELLIE. *(sotto voce)* I don't think he's ready for us to know what really goes on around here.

(**MANNY** *pretends not to hear the remark, sets down the bags, quickly goes to throw the terrace doors open.*)

MANNY. *(pitching)* You've got your own place all to your-selves out here! There's a two-bedroom suite right over the garage, all newly decorated.

NELLIE. *(crossing)* The Pool House?

MANNY. *(taking their bags, self-satisfied) Above* the pool house and *beside* the racquetball court.

JOSH. My, my, ain't this grand!

NELLIE. Ain't it! What's a racquetball court?

MANNY. *(facetiously)* Where you make racket. You'll feel right at home.

NELLIE. *(knows the put-on)* No, it's not. It's that game Nick plays.

MANNY. In his youth, perhaps.

(**MANNY** *has swept out the terrace door and disappeared around the side of the house.* **NELLIE** *and* **JOSH** *exit after him.*)

(*A moment, and* **KIT** *enters the front door, carrying a small case and waving to the limousine chauffeur…*)

KIT. *(graciously)* Thank you very, very much for our first "stretch experience" and I hope you drive us again when we leave! Happy New Year!

(*She smiles and closes the door. She's wearing gabardine slacks and a camel polo coat around her shoulders. She stops, puts down the case and looks around the room to spot the Christmas tree. She crosses to it…*)

(*quietly, to herself*) How pitiful.

(**KIT** *turns her attention to a silver framed photograph of* **WENDY** *that is sitting on the bar. She crosses to it, picks it up and studies it.* **MANNY** *enters from the terrace, sees her.* **KIT** *looks up, sees him, replaces the frame on top of the bar.*)

MANNY. *(re: picture)* I called her and asked her if she'd mind moving her things out while you were here. Actually, there wasn't much stuff – she has her own apartment. *(indicates the photograph)* She must have missed that.

KIT. Maybe she doesn't consider it her possession – it's signed, "To Manny, from Wendy, with oceans of love."

MANNY. It doesn't say "oceans," you're making that up!

(The phone rings. MANNY *goes to the niche under the stairs answer it.)*

MANNY. *(into phone)* Hello? *(forced lightly)* Oh, hi, Ma! No, the plane didn't crash! Just this very minute, I *swear...* oh, hi, Pop! Oh, you're on the cellular extension by the pool? Uh-huh, Great. Don't fall in-you could be electrocuted. *(forces a tight smile at* KIT *)* Yeah, we flew *very carefully.* Oh, they're out back unpacking. I'll get 'em to call you, but she's right here, hang on... *(covers receiver; sotto)* Pleeease!!! Do not invite them over now. Say you've got twenty-four-hour typhoid or something...

KIT. *(into phone)* Hi, there! Well...my first impression is that it's so amazingly spring-has-sprung, it's a pleasure to sneeze to flatter the pollen. Yes, it was snowing when we left. *(looks at* MANNY, *quotes Mabel)* Yes, *"real weather."* Sure. New Year's brunch at your place sounds great! *(modestly)* Oh, you're welcome, I'm just glad you liked everything. *(clears throat)* Yes...I got the blouse...It was...

MANNY. Unthinkable.

KIT. *Unexpected!* I never in my life expected what was in that...well, unique box until I saw the muttonchop sleeves! – *(incredulous)* You kept it since the fifties – the *box.* Oh, well! That's exactly why I didn't bring it – the box is a collector's item and the blouse was so hard get back in it without getting it crushed. I'd have never forgiven myself if it'd been crushed.

MANNY. *(from the background)* Crushed is what it ought to be! Crushed to death! Crushed like *The Fly's* head and claw.

KIT. *("shooing" him; warmly)* Well, I long to see you and I love you both very, very much. Bye for now! – *(hangs up)* Bernie says they can take the real weather back East and shovel it where the sun don't shine.

MANNY. What's the E.T.A. for the bagels and root canal?

KIT. Tomorrow morning at ten. They're dying to know what I think of their place.

MANNY. *(proudly, expansively re: his house)* Their place?! Well...I'm dying to know what you think of mine!

KIT. *(looking around)* Oh, Manny, it's...it's horribly marvelous.

MANNY. *(wilts)* You don't like it.

KIT. *(softer)* Listen, I know you think I'm very old-stuffed-sofa-pillow and I guess I am, but it's really... well, terribly impressive. Especially for someone like you who used to keep green bologna sandwiches in with your sox and underwear. It's awfully attractive. Honestly. *(re: the tree)* Old tannenebaum is pathetic, of course, but the house couldn't be any nicer.

MANNY. *(assuaged)* Thanks. I did the tree myself. Just in case you took me up on my offer to come out, I wanted things to look nice and Christmasey. I wanted it all to be as "perfect" as I can make it, so I had the house all done by a decorator. I know it's not your taste but...

KIT. Can't you take "yes" for an answer? I wouldn't want to stay in Southern California in anything else but a Spanish-style house. I wouldn't want any of those things we passed on the way – English Tudor, French Normandy, Greek temple, Hanzel and Gretel's cottage. I like to know where I am.

MANNY. Stop right there! I'll take that as a compliment. Come on, let me show you your room. *(He starts to pick up the bags.)* It's so strange how I find myself explaining to our children that we have separate bedrooms. It's *me*, not *them*.

KIT. *(ascending stairs)* It's on their minds, too, though. Once, Nellie's homework was to write a word with each of the letters of the alphabet. So she wrote pretty much the usual – you know, apple, boy, cat, dog, and so on. When she got to "X" do you know what she put down? Ex-husband.

(They have reached the top of the stairs. **MANNY** *bursts out laughing, suddenly stops, gasps for air, feels his heart.)*

KIT. What's the matter?

MANNY. Oh, god, when I think of those kid having little minds of their own, growing and thinking and…*twisting*, I feel like I'm going to faint. Feel my heart and don't say, *"What* heart?"

KIT. *(feels his heart)* Yes, yes, it pumping away as uncomplaining as a waterfall.

MANNY. *(trembling lip)* I think I'd better lie down and be quiet. I'll just put your things in the Sand Room and I'll be in the Sage Room.

KIT. *(incredulously)* The Sand Room, the Sage Room?

MANNY. I know it sounds like a Vegas casino, but I swear to god that's what the decorator called them. Desert colors, get it? Will you come in later and check on me?

KIT. *(nods)* Soon as I check on the "kinder" – make sure they haven't drained the pool or burned down the garage.

MANNY. *(lip-trembling whimper)* Promise to come see if *I'm* still alive.

KIT. *(nods)* Yes, I promise.

MANNY. *(indicates the terrace doors, starts up the stairs)* Go right out through there. Oh, god, Kit, how am I ever going to talk to Josh? How am I ever going to face my own son? How am I ever going to be different from my own parents?

KIT. *(heads toward terrace)* Meditate. They tell me it's an old California custom.

MANNY. That reminds me, I still have an outstanding bill at the Ashram, so maybe they've blocked my meditation privileges.

*(**KIT** laughs, goes out the terrace doors. **MANNY** continues up the stairs as dramatically as if he were on his way to the guillotine. He exits off right.)*

*(The stage is empty and silent for a moment. Then, the front door is unlocked and presently, it is opened by a very beautiful young woman in her late-twenties, dressed in slacks and wearing dark glasses. This is **WENDY**.)*

(She enters, quite unconcerned that anyone is at home. She is carrying a canvas shopping bag and goes directly to the bar, takes the framed photograph of herself and stuffs it into the bag.)

*(Momentarily, **KIT** re-enters from the terrace, sees her, stops. After a moment, **KIT** speaks...)*

KIT. Don't let me frighten you.

WENDY. *(spins around, startled, takes off glasses, recognizes **KIT**)* Oh, my god, you're here already!

KIT. Well, yes. Manny said that he had called you.

WENDY. He did. I just didn't think you'd get here so... Hello, I'm Wendy.

KIT. Yes, I recognize you from your picture. *(glances toward the bar)* Where *is* your picture?

WENDY. *(sheepishly)* In the bag. That's what I came back for. I took everything else when Manny called – but I guess I forgot the picture. I suppose that sounds deeply Freudian or something. Maybe not even so deeply. Anyway, when I finally remembered having forgotten it, I dashed right over. I didn't see Manny's car or I certainly wouldn't have...

KIT. *(rather pleased)* We came in a stretch limo. My first. I think they're brilliant – like mobile coffins – you can lie down the whole way. *(re: **WENDY**'s photograph)* There's no need to take your picture – that is, unless *you* want it removed. We've all seen it.

WENDY. *(chagrined)* The kids, too?

KIT. Oh, they know all about you! I'm *glad* there was a picture of you here. It satisfies their curiosity and besides, that's the way things are. I want them to know the facts. *Please,* do put it back. For the family's sake.

WENDY. *(after a moment)* Okay.

(She takes the picture out of the canvas shopping bag and replaces it on the bar.)

KIT. Would you like something? Some tea or coffee or a drink?

WENDY. No, thanks. Would *you?* After all, you just got here and I know where everything is. It would be easier for me to fix it.

KIT. Oh, no thanks, but that's very considerate of you to offer. *(sits on a chair, center)* Did you meet Manny on the show?

WENDY. Yes, I'm with the network.

KIT. Oh, I know. He told me. I just didn't know if you had known each other from before.

WENDY. *(sits on the couch)* No, it was when we were doing the pilot. I came on the scoring stage when he was recording the main title and I looked at him and he looked at me and…

KIT. …And you both instantly knew you were going to get in some trouble together.

WENDY. That's right. How did you know?

KIT. I know the feeling. And I know *he* knows the feeling.

WENDY. I suppose you would. Of course, I made the first move. You probably also know that's essential with Manny.

KIT. Oh, my, yes. He's much too insecure to make the first move. His precious little ego's much too fragile to ever risk a turndown. The only way he's ever had a girl was if she came on to him first. I know *I* did.

WENDY. I know *I* did. And I have no idea at all what I saw in him – he's not all that good looking, really.

KIT. Oh, he's not all that good looking at all.

WENDY. Not in a conventional way. At best, he's offbeat.

KIT. At best. Offbeat – which is a funny thing to say about a musician. Now, the fellow I'm practically engaged to is a knockout in a conventional way. Definitely on-the-beat. He's so good looking, in fact, that it really intimidated Manny when they met. I could tell.

WENDY. You mean Nick?

KIT. You know about Nick?

WENDY. Oh, god, yes! Manny never shuts up about him, he's so jealous. But I probably know less about Nick than you know about me because, let's face it, Manny has a far bigger mouth than *you* could ever have.

KIT. *(simply)* Yes. Manny's talked about you quite comprehensively.

WENDY. Honestly, he's impossible!

KIT. Totally impossible!

WENDY. He's got all the things I go for: he says he doesn't love me, he says he doesn't want a relationship, he says he certainly doesn't want to get married again, so he's perfect. It's guaranteed to fail. It's doomed from the start. I keep wondering – if I'm so aware of what I'm doing to myself, why am I doing what I'm doing to myself? I'm a reasonably attractive, reasonably intelligent person – so what do I need this shit for?

KIT. You're very beautiful and Manny says you're smart as hell.

WENDY. If I'm so smart, why'd I allow myself to get pregnant. Did he tell you that, too?

KIT. Well…

WENDY. Of course he told you that! It was probably the first thing out of his mouth!

KIT. No. I'd say, it was actually the third thing out of his mouth.

WENDY. Mind if I have a cigarette? I'll go outside to smoke it.

KIT. No, no, make yourself at home. After all, it *is* your home.

WENDY. I probably do spend more time here than I do at my own apartment.

(**WENDY** *takes a pack of cigarettes and a book of matches out of her handbag, offers one to* **KIT**.)

KIT. (*shakes her head*) Thanks. I don't smoke. Anymore. Mostly.

WENDY. Good on you, as the Australians say. Have you ever been to Australia?

KIT. No.

WENDY. We filmed a show there. Had a ball. The food was wonderful. And the drinks. Oh, would you like an Australian cigarette? They're a more like "cigarillos."

(*She begins to dig in her bag…*)

KIT. Thanks, but I'm serious about giving them up. Well, I'm *trying*. It's one of several things I'm trying.

(*Slight pause.* **WENDY** *lights up, drops the book of matches on the coffee table.*)

WENDY. (*seriously*) I don't think it would be so smart of me to have a baby. Not good for anybody at this particular moment – Manny or me or especially, *the baby*. So, I had an abortion. Not the cheeriest of weeks for it but then, not the cheeriest of tasks *any* week.

KIT. Are you all right?

WENDY. Oh, physically I'm okay, but emotionally, I'm pretty shaky. I have very complicated feelings about it. But somehow, for me, anyway, I felt I was doing the right thing for right now. I didn't tell Manny what I was planning to do while he was away. I don't know what he would have said.

(**KIT** *is silent. Another brief pause.* **WENDY** *flicks her ash into an ashtray on the coffee table.*)

(*after a moment*) You know he's still in love with you and I can see why. You seem so…sensible. And sensitive. So *real*.

KIT. Real?

WENDY. Yeah. No bullshit.

KIT. Thanks.

WENDY. Why'd you come out here?

KIT. I'm not sure. But I hope it's not like getting pregnant in the Outback.

WENDY. Do you want to get together? I mean you and Manny.

KIT. *(directly)* I guess that's what I thought I'd try to find out.

WENDY. When he asked me to take my things and stay in my apartment, I thought to myself, "Fuck *him*."

KIT. I can appreciate that. Totally.

WENDY. I thought, "This is it! I'm never coming back to this house again." – I wasn't angry at *him*, just at myself. At what I'd done to myself yet again with yet another guy. The funny thing is, now that it's over, I feel sad but it's a *good* sadness. I feel like there just might be a chance for a fresh start... *(She starts to cry, takes another drag on her cigarette.)* I'm sorry.

*(***KIT*** gets up, moves over, sits beside her on the couch and puts her arms around her.)*

KIT. It's okay.

WENDY. *(weeping)* I'm so embarrassed.

KIT. Oh, don't be. I always wanted to be able to smoke and cry at the same time – like Simone Signoret in *Room At The Top*.

WENDY. I'm sorry, but that was before my time.

KIT. *(indulgently)* Mine too. I've seen it on television.

*(***WENDY*** looks at the pink tree, begins to laugh.)*

WENDY. Is that tree the most pathetic looking thing you've ever seen?

KIT. *(laughs)* The most!

*(***MANNY*** has appeared at the top of the stairs, dressed only in his shirt [now very rumpled], jockey shorts and sox. His hair is wildly disheveled from lying down.)*

(He stops, looks down to see **KIT** *and* **WENDY** *and reacts incredulously! He can't believe he's actually seeing the two of them together – and not just talking, but laughing and hugging each other.)*

(He starts to creep down the stairs, his eyes widening, his jaw dropping further and further...)

WENDY. *(digs in her purse, finds a Kleenex)* Oh, I feel so much better now! And I don't mean just because of the good cry, though that certainly helped.

KIT. Me, too! I feel a hundred times better!

WENDY. You're *so* nice!

(Now she throws her arms about **KIT***, hugs her.* **MANNY** *is now down the stairs and coming up behind them.)*

MANNY. *(heatedly)* Pardon me, but I had no idea that you two had met!

*(***WENDY** *releases* **KIT***.)*

KIT. *(flatly)* Manny, you really must stop sneaking up on people from behind!

MANNY. Let alone had time to get all huggy-wuggy on the couch!

KIT. We're complete strangers who've know each other all our lives.

WENDY. *(laughing at the sight of* **MANNY***)* Oh, Manny, you look so funny. You've got major Bed Hair!

KIT. *(amused)* And I'd forgotten what witty knees you have! – they wrinkle just like those stupid "Smiley Faces" – Where're your pants?

MANNY. *(haughtily) Who cares?!* You both have seen me without them before! And I've seen both of you with Bed Hair! But neither of your kneecaps are anywhere as witty as mine! *(indignantly, to* **WENDY***) What are you doing here?*

KIT. *(off-handedly)* Just getting acquainted.

*(***JOSH** *runs in from the terrace where the light, by now, has gone orange and lavender with the sunset. He is in*

*a bathing suit with a beach towel wrapped around him.
His hair is wet.)*

JOSH. Mom! Mom, come here a minute… *(sees* **WENDY,**
stops) …Oh, hi! – *(dryly)* You're The Other Woman,
aren't you?

WENDY. *(tentatively)* Yes, I guess I am.

JOSH. You're even sexier looking than your picture.

KIT. *(appalled)* Oh, Josh!

> (**JOSH** *and* **WENDY** *shake hands.* **MANNY** *is incredu-
> lous.)*

WENDY. *(to* **JOSH***)* That's very sweet of you to say.

JOSH. Nice to finally meet you. I guess I'll be seeing more
of you later. Mom, come watch me do this cool new
dive I've just invented.

KIT. In a minute. Is Nell in the pool, too?

JOSH. Yeah, why don't you come in, too! It's great!

KIT. Better not leave her alone out there. *(looking outside)*
Oh, it's almost dark.

JOSH. There're colored lights everywhere-even in the palm
trees. Imagine being able to snorkel in winter! You
have all the luck, Dad!

(He runs back out the terrace doors.)

MANNY. Lucky, that's me! The luckiest little snorkeler in
the world.

WENDY. Well, I guess I'd better be going.

MANNY. *(mock gracious)* Oh, why go? I think it's so civilized
that you're here and getting acquainted with everyone
so wonderfully, so why leave now?

WENDY. Actually, I have a date and I really better start pulling myself together.

MANNY. A *date?! Who with?!*

WENDY. *(calmly)* Well, you didn't think I was going to sit at
home on New Year's Eve, did you?

MANNY. That's what *I'm* doing!

*(**WENDY** and **KIT** exchange tight, knowing smiles.)*

WENDY. *(to **KIT**)* I can see this is going to take a turn for the worse. Goodbye and thank you for being so…so….

KIT. *(sincerely, protesting)* Please. I'm just happy we got the chance to meet and talk.

*(**MANNY** stares at them slack-jawed. **NELLIE** races in from the terrace in a swimsuit, wet hair, her body wrapped in a beach towel.)*

MANNY. *(bluntly, to **NELLIE**)* Yes?! May we help you?!

NELLIE. Josh said The Other Woman was here and I just wanted to get a look.

KIT. Nell! *(**WENDY** laughs…)*

NELLIE. *(giving **WENDY** the once-over)* NOT BAD! BYE!

(She barrels back out the terrace doors.)

MANNY. *(mock calm)* I feel like this is a hallucination. A really bad trip.

KIT. Relax, Manny. No one's taking this very seriously but you.

MANNY. *(snapping at **KIT**)* Well, I *do* take it seriously! Call me old-fashioned! Call me fuddy-duddy! Call me Manny-wanny!

*(The doorbell rings. The evening light on the terrace should be gone by now. **MANNY** whips around in the direction of the front door, starts for it, stops, realizes he doesn't have on any pants. He turns back to **KIT** and **WENDY**…)*

MANNY. You two seem to be wearing the pants around here – why don't one of you answer it?!

*(**KIT** and **WENDY** look at each other.)*

KIT. *(to **WENDY**)* Well, you actually live here. I'm just a guest.

MANNY. *(to **KIT**)* Yes, you're only staying here but you live somewhere else – while she's staying somewhere else but actually lives here. Explain *that* to your mother!

WENDY. *(passing* **MANNY,** *going to the door)* Oh, go hide under your desert-colored duvet!

*(***WENDY** *opens the door and* **COLIN** *is standing there. He's forty-something, average looking, dressed in black-tie. He carries a jeroboam of Dom Perignon which has a silver bow tied around the neck of the bottle.)*

WENDY. *(brightly)* Colin! Come in!

MANNY. Oh, my, yes, come one, come all! We're having Open House. And you've dressed – you shouldn't have! *I* didn't. *(sarcastically)* I thought you always called before you dropped in. I thought it was one of your unwritten rules.

*(***COLIN** *is a bit thrown by what he has walked into, but manages it smoothly.)*

COLIN. I could go to my car phone if it'll keep my record unblemished. Am I getting you at an awkward time?

MANNY. An *awkward time*? No, nooo! Why would you think that?

COLIN. Well, I'm only staying a minute, I'm on my way to…

MANNY. No, no, no, come in and stay as long as you like!

(He pulls **COLIN** *into the room.)*

WENDY. *(shuts the door)* Hi Collie!

COLIN. Wendola! You look positively sleek with happiness.

WENDY. Thanks. I think I am, rather.

MANNY. *(to* **COLIN***)* Allow me to introduce my wife – uh, my ex-wife!

*(***COLIN** *goes to* **KIT,** *shakes her hand warmly.)*

COLIN. *(dryly)* Welcome to our city.

KIT. *(to* **COLIN***)* I understand we almost don't need an introduction.

COLIN. He must have mentioned me, too.

KIT. *(with meaning)* Not…in as intimate detail, I don't believe.

COLIN. Well, I hope you won't hold it against me. I loved everything I heard about you.

KIT. I like what I heard about you, too.

MANNY. *(to* **WENDY***)* Isn't that *sweet*? They're instant old friends, too! I seem to be the only outsider!

COLIN. *(hands* **MANNY** *the jeroboam)* Here. I thought this might come in handy later this evening.

KIT. *(brightly)* How lovely!

MANNY. Isn't it lovely?! Chilled, too! See, Kit, I told you he was thoughtful.

WENDY. I'm leaving before one drop of alcohol is consumed.

   (to **KIT** *re: her photograph)*

   – If you don't mind, I think I will take that after all.

KIT. I understand perfectly.

   *(***WENDY** *goes to the bar, takes the picture, stuffs in back in the canvas shopping bag.)*

MANNY. *(to* **WENDY***)* What are you doing?!

WENDY. Never mind, Manny.

MANNY. *(to* **KIT***)* Maybe *you'll* explain since you understand so much!

KIT. I think she's leaving you.

   *(***JOSH** *comes in from the kitchen door, wearing a terry cloth robe, drying his hair with a small towel.)*

JOSH. Excuse me, Mom, but Nell's hungry. What are we gonna do about dinner?

KIT. I don't know yet. Is there something in the fridge to tide you over?

JOSH. Not much. Some diet soda and a pound of caviar. Gift wrapped.

MANNY. *(generally)* A Christmas present from my agent.

WENDY. *(apologetically)* Oh, I'm afraid I cleaned out the fridge – I didn't want things to spoil while Manny was away.

MANNY. *(to* **JOSH***)* Well, how about some diet soda and caviar?

COLIN. *(to* **KIT***)* I could drive you to the market.

WENDY. No, *I* will. It's my fault.

MANNY. *(to* **WENDY** *and* **COLIN***)* Why don't the two of you fight over it!

KIT. *(appreciative, but negative)* Thank you both, but we'll figure something out...

JOSH. Could we go out for pizza?

WENDY. Oh, there's a terrific pizza place right on Beverly Drive. And they deliver fast. Shall I call?

MANNY. *(to* **WENDY***)* Please don't! You've been helpful enough! *(to* **JOSH***, bluntly)* We'll figure out what and where you'll *eat* as soon as the guests get out of here!

JOSH. What's eating you, Dad? *(to all)* Excuse me.

*(***JOSH*** exits out the terrace doors.* **WENDY** *turns to* **KIT***.)*

WENDY. Goodbye, Kit, and thanks.

KIT. No need to thank me. It was nothing. Really.

WENDY. *(goes to* **COLIN***)* Bye, Collie.

COLIN. *(kisses* **WENDY** *on the cheek)* Happy New Year.

WENDY. *(goes to* **MANNY***)* So long, Manny. Here's your house key. Call me after your family leaves. We ought to have a serious chat about how to proceed with our lives next year – which is tomorrow.

*(***WENDY*** goes out the front door and closes it.* **MANNY** *turns back to* **KIT** *and* **COLIN***.)*

COLIN. *(incredulously)* Is that a pink tree?

MANNY. Yes, and make something of it!

COLIN. How about a fire?

*(***KIT*** laughs.* **MANNY** *boils.)*

KIT. *(to* **COLIN***, forced lightly)* I know it sounds weird, but that tree reminds me of Maureen O'Hara. *(touches her hair)* Maybe it's because she was the first redhead to have the courage to wear pink. Not that shade of pink, of course.

COLIN. *(charmingly)* You have very lovely red hair.

KIT. *(diffidently)* And the freckles to match, I'm afraid – but thank you.

MANNY. *(with an edge)* If I may interrupt, I think I'll slip into something a little more uncomfortable and order a pizza for my children.

*(**MANNY** shoves the bottle of Dom Perignon into **KIT**'s hands, turns and pounds up the stairs. When he is out of sight, **KIT** turns to **COLIN**.)*

KIT. Why wait for midnight? Why not open this heavenly bottle and have a cup of kindness right now?

COLIN. Why not?

KIT. Will you do the honors?

COLIN. I'd be honored to do the honors.

*(**KIT** hands **COLIN** the bottle. He starts to untwist the wire around the cork.)*

KIT. I'll get two lovely long-stem glasses…

(She heads behind the bar when the doorbell rings.)

COLIN. *(to **KIT**)* They can't deliver that fast!

*(**KIT** has taken two glasses from a shelf and placed them on the counter top. She goes to the front door. **COLIN** crosses behind the bar, gets a towel, starts to pull the cork.)*

*(**KIT** opens the miniature door peephole, looks out, reacts.)*

KIT. *(astounded)* Oh, my!

COLIN. *(agog)* You mean it *is* the pizza man?!

KIT. I don't quite know who or *what* it is!

(She opens the door, steps outside, out of sight.)

KIT. *(offstage)* Good evening! Thank you, very much! They're…they're wonderful!

(A moment, and through the front door there begins to emerge an enormous bouquet of helium-filled rubber balloons. There must be three dozen of them in silver and gold and white, tied with the same colored ribbons,

gathered and weighted with a silver top-hat filled with noise-makers and an envelope.)

(COLIN is arrested by the sight, stops what he's doing as KIT shuts the door and "floats" back into the room.)

COLIN. Well! That's pretty splendid! Who'd send Manny…?

KIT. *(placing the top hat on the bar)* No, they're not for Manny – they're for *me*! There's a card here in the hat with my name on it! *(She tears open the envelope and reads the card.)* Ohh, how sweet! They're from a friend in Connecticut.

COLIN. "Good goods"?

KIT. *(reacts) Honestly!* Manny's tongue should be cut out. Manny said, rather rudely, that Nick looks like he's been delivering balloons all his life. And Josh heard him and told Nick.

COLIN. It's nice that Nick has a sense of humor about Manny's sense of humor. How'd Nick feel about your coming out here?

KIT. Well, he wasn't laughing.

COLIN. No one has that much of a sense of humor.

KIT. But he was very understanding. At least, he tried very hard to be understanding.

COLIN. He's in love with you. He'll try anything.

(COLIN pops the cork.)

KIT. Oh, what a glorious sound!

COLIN. *(pours, hands her a glass)* I can't think of anything clever to say except you're everything I'd imagined and much, much more.

KIT. That's clever enough for this redhead.

COLIN. Cheers!

KIT. Cheers!

*(They clink glasses and drink as **MANNY** comes down the stairs. He has changed into a black silk shirt and a pair of black velour trousers. He sees the bouquet of balloons.)*

MANNY. *(to* **COLIN***)* What's *that*?!

COLIN. Balloons. From her lover, The Balloon Man. You remember him.

KIT. Sweet of Nick, don't you think?

MANNY. *(to* **COLIN***)* You ought to see this creep. So WASP he makes *you* look hamish. Really got a broom up his ass.

*(***MANNY*** picks up the card, but* **KIT** *snaps it out of his hand...)*

KIT. I believe that has my name on it.

MANNY. It's still my name, too. *(to* **COLIN***)* I see we're not waiting for midnight to dive into the shampoo.

COLIN. Why stand on ceremony?

MANNY. Why stand on ceremony when you can stand on your ear? Why don't we break out the gift-wrapped caviar!

COLIN. Why not?!

*(***COLIN*** gets another glass for* **MANNY***.)*

(to **MANNY***)* Here. Have a bit of the bubbly to take the cramp out of your soul.

*(***MANNY*** tosses the card back into the hat with disgust, holds up a hand to* **COLIN** *before he pours.)*

MANNY. None for me, thanks. I have my own method for getting a glow on.

*(***MANNY*** turns and exits to the kitchen.* **COLIN** *picks up a steel trash basket and begins to prepare it with ice from the machine.)*

COLIN. I'm afraid the real ice bucket isn't going to do the trick. Anyway, when you have Italian trash baskets from Ogetti, who could ask for anything more?

KIT. *(holding her glass)* God, isn't champagne wonderful?! One should really be dressed like you, Colin, to drink champagne on New Year's Eve!

COLIN. *(re: his watch)* Oh, look at the time!

KIT. *(disappointed)* Aw, you're not going already, are you?

COLIN. Don't you want me to?

KIT. Not if you don't want to.

COLIN. I don't want to go and I don't want to go to the party anyway. *(smiles)* Maybe I'll just call and cancel.

(**MANNY** *returns with the tin of caviar in one hand and a caviar bowl with a place for crushed ice, in the other.*)

MANNY. *(general announcement)* Toast triangles with the crusts trimmed, coming up!

(**COLIN** *is placing the jeroboam of Dom Perignon in trash basket.*)

MANNY. *(extending the caviar bowl to* **COLIN**) Here, put some ice in this thing.

COLIN. *(taking the bowl)* What do you know, a proper caviar server! I'm impressed.

MANNY. Yeah, well, we run a tight ship! Which reminds me, why are you using my imported Italian trash can as an ice bucket?

COLIN. It's jeroboam size.

MANNY. *(re: trash basket)* Ah, well as you see, it certainly wasn't chock-full of discarded masterpieces of musical composition.

COLIN. Blocked again?

MANNY. From the moment I laid eyes on The Balloon Man, my bowels blocked and locked and threw away the key.

COLIN. *(re: champagne)* A little of this will keep you as regular as your alimony checks.

(**MANNY** *exits to the kitchen, giving* **COLIN** *a look en route.*)

KIT. *(toying with the card)* Nick really does possess the most outstanding qualities and character.

COLIN. I'm sure he deserves the Nobel Prize for being noble – but do you love him?

KIT. *(picks up her champagne)* In my own…very warm and… respectful way.

COLIN. *(refilling her glass)* Sounds rather fraternal.

KIT. Maybe so. I never had a brother, more's the pity. Thanks.

COLIN. Neither did I. Nor a sister, for that matter. But that's how I'd like to feel toward one if I had.

KIT. You're an only child?

COLIN. 'Fraid so.

KIT. So's Manny.

COLIN. Oh, yes, I know. *(crossing to the coffee table)* I think there's so much to be profited from sibling rivalry. So many of the slings and arrows of childhood can be shared. And that can come in very handy later in life.

KIT. I'm not so sure. I have one sister and I think I'd rather *get* her with a sling and arrow, rather than *share* one with her.

COLIN. *(laughs)* Is she older or younger?

KIT. A year younger. She lives and works in Paris. She's a correspondent for CNN.

COLIN. Oh, yes, I've seen her on TV. Manny told me she was your sister – rather, *his* sister-in-law.

KIT. Yes, she was "The Right One" – the one who, "Did something with her life." I'm the one who, as my mother puts it: "Never did anything but marry an exotic."

*(**MANNY** swings in from the kitchen, a basket of toast triangles in hand.)*

MANNY. *(to **COLIN**)* And you know what she means by "exotic," don't you?

(He puts the toast on the bar.)

MANNY. Toast isosceles! *(to **KIT**)* *Perfect* enough for you?

KIT. *(ignores the question, picks up last remark)* My mother means you were an unwashed, uncombed, filthy, long-haired, pot-head from the dregs of the seventies.

MANNY. She *means* I'm Jewish.

KIT. *She does not!*

MANNY. *(to* **KIT***)* She doesn't say that, but that's what she means.

KIT. My mother is a lot of horrendous things, Manny, but what she is *not* is a bigot!

MANNY. I didn't say she was a bigot. She's just Episcopalian.

(He turns and exits to the kitchen.)

KIT. *(to* **COLIN***)* She *is* pretty white bread.

COLIN. Mine too. Born and bred white bread.

KIT. Boston is it?

COLIN. No, but I went to school there. Charleston.

KIT. God, you don't sound it.

COLIN. Didn't spend too much time there. Always in school somewhere. Boarding school. Prep school. You get the picture.

KIT. Oh, yes. Me, too. Actually, I'm considering sending Josh to boarding school, but I don't want him to misunderstand. I don't want him to think because he's gotten into trouble lately, I'm trying to punish him by shipping him out.

COLIN. My two boys are at a wonderful place in Colorado. I could tell you about it.

KIT. *(crossing to him)* Oh, please do. How old are they?

COLIN. Sixteen and fifteen. God, I can't believe I said that. They're getting old and I'm getting older.

KIT. Josh is going to be seventeen on his next birthday. I feel like I'm a hundred.

COLIN. You look about seventeen yourself

KIT. You *are* from the south. That's gotta be what they call gallantry.

COLIN. I mean it.

KIT. Thanks. I didn't know you'd been married.

COLIN. I suppose Manny only told you about Jim.

KIT. Yes, and he didn't even tell me his name – he just referred to him as "Colin's friend." – I'm very sorry. I know that's not enough, but I am sorry.

COLIN. Thanks.

(**MANNY** *breezes in.*)

MANNY. What's going on in here behind my back? And I'm not being paranoid.

COLIN. It's not behind your back, it's under your nose.

MANNY. *(to* **KIT***)* Did he tell you he's Episcopalian, too? A Carolinian Episcopalian. *(sings)* "Nothin' could be finer than to integrate a diner in the morn-o-orn-nin'!"

COLIN. *(to* **KIT***)* Well, I was baptized one, but I'm really nothing.

MANNY. Just a zero? I didn't know you had such a low self-esteem.

KIT. What have you been smoking in the kitchen?

COLIN. It sho' ain't ham, honey!

MANNY. It's not behind your back, it's under your nose!

(**MANNY** *produces a joint from his breast pocket, extends it to* **KIT**. *She pushes it away.*)

KIT. No thanks. My cup runneth under.

(She goes to refill her glass.)

MANNY. *(offers the joint to* **COLIN***)* How 'bout you, suh?

COLIN. *(holds up his glass if champagne)* Ah think ah'll jes' sip on mah bourbon and branch water.

MANNY. *(to* **KIT***)* When you say you've stopped smoking – I thought you meant cigarettes.

KIT. I *did* mean cigarettes. I'm just not in the mood.

MANNY. What the matter, afraid it's gonna get you all hot and bothered? All reefer madness and sex-crazed?

KIT. *(with exhausted indulgence)* Yes, Manny, that's *just* what I was afraid of.

MANNY. *(re:* **KIT** *and* **COLIN***)* Am I interrupting something here? I get the feeling I've just sorta stepped on my cock.

COLIN. *(re: joint)* How much of that stuff have you had?

MANNY. *(snapping mildly at* **COLIN***)* I am not getting paranoid, if that's what you're implying. What were you two discussing in here – The Life and Times of Manny Boy?

KIT. Incredible as it may seem, your name was never mentioned.

MANNY. Well, then maybe what you have to say to each other is not for my ears. Maybe I should just leave. Fold my petals and drop my tent.

COLIN. Just don't drop your pants.

KIT. *(to* **COLIN***, laughs)* Oh, you've caught that act, have you?

COLIN. *(nods, to* **KIT***)* Pretty, isn't it?

MANNY. *I'm not budging.*

KIT. *(to* **COLIN***)* Anyway, as I was saying…

MANNY. *(mock huffily)* Before you were so rudely interrupted.

KIT. …we've got to do something about Josh. The first thing is that I want him to see some kind of therapist.

MANNY. Christ, I'm not even finished with analysis myself and my son is already starting!

KIT. I didn't know you were seeing a doctor.

MANNY. Off and on. I'm not that sick, you know. I mean, *you* may think I am… *(to* **COLIN***)* …and *you* may think I am, but I'm not!

KIT. I think it's great that you're seeing someone. I wish you'd done it years ago. I wish *I'd* done it years ago.

COLIN. I saw someone for a while, right after Jim died. It helped a lot.

KIT. I'm sure it would help Josh a lot, too. I hope you, agree, Manny.

MANNY. Oh, I'm all *for* it. I just don't want to *pay* for it, that's all. How do poor people pay for it?

COLIN. I don't know any poor people who are seeing analysts.

(**COLIN** *takes the champagne bottle out of the bucket…*)

COLIN. *(to* **KIT***)* A tad more?

KIT. *(extends her glass cheerfully)* A tad, thank you. *(moves to the foot of the stairs…)* I should go up and get into a gown – not a dress, mind you, but a gown – something on the bias – after all, this *is* Hollywood – and make an entrance down the stairs and sweep over to the door and stand with the knob in the small of my back… *(moves to stand with her back against the front door)* And sweep over to the fireplace and stand, staring soulfully into the fire… *(She glides to the fireplace, looking into an unlit pile of logs.)* Of course, there should be a fire for me to stare soulfully into.

COLIN. *(smiling, charmed)* That should be easy enough to arrange.

KIT. You mean ignite the tree or are these gas logs?

(**MANNY** *jumps up and goes to the fireplace.*)

MANNY. *Don't touch that tree!* And those are not gas logs! Those are *real* logs. There is, however, a gas starter – just to make life a teensy-weensy bit easier than rubbing two sticks together – the way you do it way back east in the land of no bullshit!

KIT. *(calmly)* I have a gas starter, way back east in the land of no bullshit. You're so defensive!

(**MANNY** *has bent to turn on the gas starter which ignites the fire.*)

MANNY. *(stands, to* **KIT***)* You were completely born out of your generation, weren't you? You were really born to do *The Continental*, weren't you? You and Rogers and Astaire.

COLIN. Astaire and Rogers. Let's get the billing right.

MANNY. *(an eye-roll)* Oh, god, yes, let's!

(**KIT** *crosses to* **COLIN** *at the bar.*)

KIT. Love, love, *love* Rogers and Astaire.

COLIN. Well, who doesn't?

KIT. *(flatly) Manny* doesn't.

(**KIT** *holds out her empty glass and* **COLIN** *refills it.*)

MANNY. See, I told you you'd like each other. I knew you'd have all that old shit in common.

KIT. *(entre nous, to* **COLIN***)* Don't mind *him.*

COLIN. *(refilling his glass)* Oh, I don't mind him at all.

KIT. *(to* **COLIN***, enthusiastically)* I saw a marquee once – honest to god – that said, "Fred and Ginger in Irving's *Top Hat*" – !!!

COLIN. N-ooo!

KIT. I swear!

COLIN. How wonderful!

KIT. I think that about says it, don't you?

COLIN. I think that about does!

(*They both break up.*)

MANNY. *(grimly) About says what?!*

(**KIT** *and* **COLIN** *stop laughing, turn to look at him blankly.*)

MANNY. I hate all that old crap! I hate wallowing in nostalgia. I hate anything that's "avec schmaltz"!

COLIN. You're afraid of feeling, Manny. You're afraid of sentiment. You confuse it with sentimentality.

MANNY. *(snakily)* I didn't know you'd be interested in coming on with my wife.

COLIN. *(calmly)* Not even with your *ex*-wife. And one more remark like that and I'll hit you with this jeroboam right in your big, expensive teeth!

KIT. Now, this is no way for best friends to act on the last day of the year!

COLIN. Oh, we're not going to fight. Manny doesn't like confrontations.

KIT. No, but he likes to provoke them.

COLIN. Yeah, then tuck his tail and run. Actually, Manny doesn't know too much about friendship, so we're hardly best anything. He never calls unless he wants something. He never really talks to me unless it's about himself.

MANNY. What are friends for?

COLIN. You don't know the meaning of give and take. All you know is take. When somebody else is in trouble you are nowhere to be found.

MANNY. I wish I were nowhere to be found right this minute!

COLIN. Sorry, but this time, I'm the one who's going to walk. *(drains glass, turns to* KIT; *softly)* I don't know what to say to you. I…

KIT. *(gently)* It's all right. Good night, Colin, and thank you.

MANNY. *(interrupting)* I know what you're talking about.

COLIN. What?

MANNY. You're talking about the night Jim died.

COLIN. Jim and I were real, true friends, Manny. Not just lovers – best friends. It happens when you hang in with each other long enough, surviving what life has in store for you. And the night he died is the night I needed another friend – and I thought it was you. I thought that's what we called ourselves. I thought that's why I listened to your story hours on end, days on end, months…

*(*MANNY *is not only silent, he's almost catatonic. He doesn't move, just sits and stares into space.)*

You're not a friend, Manny. You're not someone I could call in the middle of the night if I needed help – because I don't know if you'd be there for me. I don't think you would be.

*(*MANNY *doesn't confirm or deny the statement, just remains totally still.* KIT *is completely aware of this, dividing her attention between what* COLIN *is saying and its effect on* MANNY.)*

COLIN. *(cont.)* I needed you once – the night Jim died and you weren't there for me. It wasn't in the middle of the night when I called – it was just about this time – and I was drunk. Oh, I was *very* drunk. Sloppy, maudlin, full of self-pity and *desperate*. It was clear from the moment I arrived. You were distant and cold – rude, almost, because I had called on the phone, drunk, *begging* to come over and talk to you. Here it was, the test of our friendship. I needed you and you weren't there. I thought I'd never forgive you for that, but I have. Because in spite of everything I think about you, I think there's something to you.

(A long moment, then **MANNY** *slowly gets up.)*

MANNY. You wanted something else and you won't admit it.

*(***MANNY*** *crosses to the front door, goes out, closing it behind him. After a moment,* **COLIN** *turns to* **KIT**.*)*

COLIN. Would you like to come to the party with me?

KIT. I honestly don't like parties. And tonight of all nights, I don't want to be pretending I'm having a good time when I'm not.

COLIN. How about if I try to book a table somewhere? It's late in the day, but there're a few head waiters that know me.

KIT. *(thinks for a moment)* Okay. We can't leave before the pizza comes. And you'll have to wait while I change and say goodnight to the kids.

COLIN. I'd be delighted to wait as long as you like.

KIT. Have another glass of your gorgeous champagne. You look a bit white-lipped and I don't wonder.

COLIN. *(re: champagne)* I think I'll do that very thing.

(They look at each other a moment.)

KIT. *(simply)* Are you in love with Manny?

COLIN. I thought I was once. And for the longest time, I kidded myself into thinking something was possible. As someone once said, "When the wrong man comes along, I'll know him." Besides everything else, Manny is hopelessly straight.

KIT. *(nods)* You don't have to tell *me*. But enough about Manny, it's *you* who concerns me.

COLIN. *(nods sardonically)* Because we have something in common. *(directly)* Well, it's nice to know I now have a friend who understands.

KIT. *(smiles)* Thank you, Colin. I feel the same way.

COLIN. Manny was right about what I really wanted from him the night my friend died. I wanted physical love. But I had wanted it on so many nights that I now wonder if my friend's death made the need that night any more special than any other night – or if I was just drunk and dramatizing, using Jim's death to try to get what I really wanted. Because, after all, it was Manny I loved.

KIT. I don't suppose you'll ever know.

COLIN. At any rate, it was clear that if it wasn't going to happen that night – then it was never going to happen. I think, for me, that realization was the end of our friendship in a special, idiosyncratic, no-holds-barred way, and the start of something ordinary. Something true and perfectly honorable – just nothing unique.

KIT. I think you underestimate true, honorable friendship. I think it is unique and not ordinary, at all.

*(**COLIN** relishes **KIT**'s sympathetic response)*

– Maybe Manny's just not who or what you need him to be, Colin. Maybe he's not what you thought he was or even what he allowed you to believe.

COLIN. You're probably right.

KIT. Creative people are so narcissistic that attention in any form is so welcome, they take it from anyone and anywhere they can get it. Adoration, recognition, validation…well!…They beg for it like dogs at a table. They wag their tails. They whine. They flirt for it. Outrageously. With anyone.

COLIN. Yeah. Trouble is, they just take and take and take and then they just walk away.

KIT. *(after a moment)* Colin…why do you want something you can't have?

COLIN. Kit…why do you want something you don't want?

(a slight pause)

KIT. *(smiles faintly)* It won't take me a minute to change.

*(**KIT** turns and goes out the terrace doors. **COLIN** goes to the wine bucket, refills his glass, goes to the telephone, picks it up, starts to call the restaurant.)*

(The curtain doesn't not come down, but the sound of cheering comes over the house speakers as the light cross fade to…)

Scene Two

(Shortly after midnight. The lighting is somewhat softer and moodier than before. A few lamps have been turned off and the embers in the hearth cast a warm, cozy glow over the room.)

*(***JOSH***, dressed in pajamas and a robe, is sitting on his knees in front of the TV with the volume turned up. An announcer's voice is reporting the events of the New Year's celebration, straining above the revelers.)*

*(One of the terrace doors is opened and ***MANNY*** comes inside. He sees ***JOSH***, stops. ***JOSH*** turns to see him, quickly turns off the news report and gets up.)*

MANNY. You don't have to turn it off.

JOSH. I already saw what I wanted to see.

MANNY. What was that?

JOSH. The countdown.

MANNY. Five, four, three, two, one…Haaappp!-peenooyeer!

JOSH. *(tentatively)* It's really exciting – time running out… tick, tick, tick, going, going, gone…and bammo, it's a whole 'nother year.

MANNY. *(without expression)* Yeah, tick, tick, tick…bammo.

JOSH. I was just writing the new date on a piece of paper and it looks so weird. I can't explain it.

MANNY. I know what you mean. It's always March before I put the right date on a check.

JOSH. That happens to me in school, too.

MANNY. *(feeble attempt)* You write checks in school?

*(***JOSH*** laughs cautiously, releasing a bit of nervous tension.)*

MANNY. I'm surprised to find you up. I didn't see any lights over the garage. I thought everybody was asleep.

JOSH. The trip and all that swimming really knocked Nell out.

MANNY. What about you?

JOSH. I still couldn't sleep.

(Brief pause. **MANNY** *glances upstairs.)*

JOSH. Mom went out with your friend.

MANNY. Oh.

JOSH. She got all dressed up and he took her someplace fancy.

MANNY. Probably the party he was invited to.

JOSH. You know Mom doesn't like parties. They went to a restaurant.

*(***JOSH** *goes to the phone, picks up a pad, crosses to hand it to* **MANNY.***)*

She left the number like she always does – in case someone breaks their neck. Ever heard of this place?

MANNY. Ohh, yes. You're right – very fancy.

JOSH. Fancy-schmancy?

MANNY. Yeah, you need a blood test to get in.

(brief pause.)

JOSH. Where'd *you* go? To a party?

MANNY. No, no, I…just went for a drive.

JOSH. By yourself?

MANNY. Yeah.

JOSH. *(looks at balloons)* Where'd the balloons come from?

MANNY. Nick sent them.

JOSH. *(after a moment)* You and Mom had a fight, didn't you?

MANNY. No, we didn't have a fight.

JOSH. I thought maybe you did. I mean, it's pretty weird to come all the way to California for New Year's and you go for a drive and she goes out with a stranger.

MANNY. I guess it is pretty weird. I guess I'm a pretty weird dad.

JOSH. Not as crazy as some.

MANNY. Thanks.

JOSH. Some of my friends have really sick parents. You're nowhere near that sick.

MANNY. Thanks. How…how sick am I? I mean, as a dad… as a parent? In your opinion.

JOSH. *(reluctantly)* Ohh, I don't know…

MANNY. I mean, tell me about *me*. I want to hear – I'd like to hear.

JOSH. I don't know…I…I… *(turns away)* I don't want to talk about it, okay? I'm going to bed.

*(**JOSH** starts toward the terrace doors.)*

MANNY. *(quickly)* Oh, Josh, don't go to bed yet. Stay here for a moment. Please? Stay here and talk to me?

*(**JOSH** hesitates, doesn't turn back, doesn't look at **MANNY**.)*

How's…how's your friend?

*(**JOSH** folds his arms, doesn't speak for a moment…)*

JOSH. What friend?

MANNY. The one who was in the accident with you.

*(**JOSH** slowly unfolds his arms, turns to **MANNY**.)*

JOSH. Mom told you about that?

MANNY. *(nods)* She was very worried. She is very worried.

JOSH. *(puts hands in pockets, looks at floor)* I figured she'd tell you, but I didn't know if she had or not because you never said anything. But then, that's just your way.

MANNY. *(directly)* What do you mean, "my way" – ?

JOSH. *(weakly)* The way you are.

MANNY. *(pressing him)* How do you mean?

*(**JOSH** doesn't answer.)*

Can you kinda fill me in on that?

(no answer)

You mean my…you mean…

*(**JOSH** turns away. Silence.)*

MANNY. *(cont.)* You mean the way I do what you're doing right now?

(Still no answer. **JOSH** *moves over by the TV.)*

Oh, Josh…you remind me so much of me. And for your sake, I'm truly sorry. I really don't want you to grow up with my bad qualities.

*(***JOSH** *turns on the television. The announcer's voice comes on…)*

…I…I'm really sorry for what…

*(***JOSH** *turns up the volume. The sound of the hysterical mob becomes louder…)*

…I know I haven't always been there for you. And I regret that. I deeply regret it and I hope it's not too late to make up for…

*(***JOSH** *turns the volume louder…)*

…When you were little, I don't know if you remember something you said. Something you said about me. You said, "Who is that man who lives with us?"

*(***JOSH** *turns the volume all the way up. The sound is deafening.)*

(over the noise) Who is that man who lives with us?! And now *I'd* like to know, if it's not too late, who my own son is?!! Who is this son I'm living with?!

*(***JOSH** *kicks the TV off button with his foot. The sound ceases.)*

JOSH. *(angrily)* You don't live with me! You never have! And I don't mean just under one roof. Even when we lived together you weren't there. *You were never there!*

MANNY. I know. I know. And I'm sorry. I want to be there. I want to be there for you. Even if you live in the east and I live in the west – I want you to know I'm there for you. Always. In spite of distance, in spite of any-thing. And I want us to try to talk to each other…to try to communicate.

(MANNY has come over to JOSH, reaches out, puts his hand on the boy's shoulder. Suddenly, JOSH wheels around and starts violently beating MANNY on the chest and arms. MANNY's hands go up defensively, but he allows JOSH to play this out, to exhaust himself until he stops and collapses in tears. MANNY puts his arms about JOSH and hold him as he continues to sob.)

(A moment, and JOSH pulls himself together and steps back from MANNY.)

JOSH. Goodnight.

MANNY. Goodnight, son.

JOSH. I hope...I hope we have a happy new year.

MANNY. I'm going to try to make it that way. I'm gonna try to do my best.

JOSH. *(quietly)* Me, too.

(JOSH goes to the terrace doors and exits. MANNY watches him. After a moment, he begins to whistle the tune to "Let's Face The Music And Dance." He sings a few lines from the song.*)

(MANNY looks at his hands. They are trembling.)

(The front door is opened and KIT enters. She looks ravishing. She's dressed in a chic, short black dress with a skirt that "moves," showing, for the first time, her beautiful legs and feet in high heel pumps. The only jewelry she has on are NICK's diamond earrings.)

(KIT doesn't see MANNY. She closes the door and starts to go up the stairs...)

MANNY. You didn't call to cancel.

(KIT stops halfway up the stairs, turns to look down at MANNY.)

KIT. We didn't have a date, to my recollection.

MANNY. You didn't call to find out if we did have one, and if we did, to cancel. It just isn't done. I'm extremely hurt.

---

*Please see Music Use Note on Page 3

KIT. Oh, Manny, it's too late in the evening – too early in the year, to start up with your…

(She breaks off, continues up a few steps. **MANNY** *comes to the bottom of the stairs.)*

MANNY. *You are staying in my house. You are my houseguest.* And I think it's a pretty rude and inconsiderate thing for a house guest to do.

KIT. *(stops, turns, slowly descends the stairs)* I think it's a pretty rude and inconsiderate thing for a host to do – behave like a brat and walk out, leave his guest and his house-guest high and dry.

MANNY. *(crosses center)* Even after the floor had been thoroughly wiped up with the host?

KIT. You asked for it.

MANNY. I left you high, but hardly dry.

*(***KIT** *goes to take it cigarette from the box on coffee table, looks at the brand…)*

KIT. Pardon me, while I read your cigarettes.

MANNY. *(seriously)* I am hurt, damn it! By him and by you.

KIT. *(passes him, crossing to bar)* Are you going to sulk?

(She investigates the cigarette box on the bar for another make.)

MANNY. If I want to! Where's your escort?

KIT. My escort escorted me to the door and then escorted himself home.

MANNY. Where'd he take you – some gay bar?

KIT. *(finds a cigarette)* Ah, my brand! *(Suddenly, she puts the cigarette back, shuts the lid firmly.)* Nope, Katie is going to be strong this year.

MANNY. He kissed you goodnight, of course. Kissy-wissy, cheeky-weeky.

KIT. No, Manny, we kissed each other goodnight. And not in the air and not on the cheeks and not, as you would so attractively put it – a big wet toilet plunger. Just a very dear, sincere kiss. *(a moment, then almost to herself)* Lovely man.

MANNY. Oh, yes, splendid chap, sterling fellow – most loyal and devoted friend any shit like me ever cared to let down. I knew the two of you would like each other. I just didn't know you'd like each other so much.

KIT. Yeah…well…we liked each other a lot.

MANNY. What is it with you and him?! I've never seen you respond to anyone like that right off the bat – even *me*! It was a month before I could get you to look me in the eye, let alone the rest of it.

KIT. *Wrong*, Manny! I was in bed with you long before I ever looked you in the eye!

MANNY. He waltzed in and whammo! – Instant eye contact and ten minutes later you're doing the foreplay two-step, Fred-and-Ginger style! Did I get the billing right?

KIT. *(incredulous realization)* You're jealous!

*(**KIT** laughs to herself…)*

MANNY. *(looking at his watch)* Do you know what time it is?

KIT. *(picks up a balloon which has sagged to the floor)* Sometime after midnight. I know that because I had champagne at midnight.

(She gives the balloon a little deliberate kick and it bounces away.)

MANNY. You had champagne *before* midnight, too!

KIT. *(crosses to bar)* Not much. Oh, look, there's some left. How about a tad?

MANNY. No, thank you.

KIT. *(pouring herself a glass)* You know, I really quite like this stuff. I mean, for a person who doesn't like to drink, really.

MANNY. *(looking at her)* For a person who doesn't like to dress, really – doesn't like to go on in public – doesn't like parties, loves their precious privacy, you certainly *have* changed. And I don't mean just your clothes!

KIT. *(draining her glass, pouring another)* I'm a late bloomer. And when at last I bloom, *watch out*!

*(**KIT** belches. Quickly covers her mouth, giggles.)*

MANNY. I feel like I don't know who the fuck you are, any-more!

KIT. *(confronting him)* When did you ever?! I *always* liked pretty clothes. And I always like putting them on when there was something to put them on for. Or *someone.* And I like taking them off, too. When there was something or someone to take them off for!

MANNY. You're pissed!

KIT. *(coolly)* Not really. Oh, I probably shouldn't operate any heavy machinery.

MANNY. You've had too much Christmas!

KIT. *(She has another sip.)* I'll have a non-stop, coast-to-coast headache tomorrow, but what the hell! I've always relished the special occasion, have I not?

MANNY. And this, I take it, is some special, special occasion?

KIT. You got it! You *so* got it! It isn't the way I thought it was going to be. It isn't why I packed this dress in so many reams of tissue paper I had to pay air freight! But tonight *is* an occasion! This *marks* something. This puts a period to a period of my life, if you catch my drift.

MANNY. Sounds like you didn't have a very good time.

KIT. That's what you'd like to think, I know! I know you, Manny – you have a shitty evening, so you want everyone else to, as well.

MANNY. You mean I didn't manage to ruin things after all?

KIT. Not in the least! In fact, you caused me to have one of the most pleasurable evenings I've had in a long, long, *very* long time! And, by the way, I still hate parties! *Hate 'em like rat remover*!

MANNY. Just the ones *I* took you to.

KIT. But as long as I can be in the middle of the melee with one person I really like, having a party all our own. Then it's fun!

*(She has picked up a noisemaker out of the silver top hot and blows it. It rolls out, extending almost to the tip of **MANNY**'s nose, makes a noise and rolls back.)*

MANNY. You're all wound-up tonight, aren't you? Wound-up like a goddamn Rolex!

KIT. Yeah, a gold Rolex, a *solid gold* Rolex in your particular *case*, which I happened to notice! And also in your particular case – a solid leather Gucci case with your initials on it – I also happened to notice a Louis Cartier tank watch.

MANNY. Go on, say it! Gone Rodeo Drive! Status Symbol Sam, that's me! That's what I clang together to make beautiful music to make beautiful money to pay your beautiful bills! My gold symbols and my gold balls!

KIT. *Solid* gold balls, if you please! Solid *monogrammed* gold balls! I rather liked the tank watch.

MANNY. *(heatedly)* I love 'em all! And I love the Springs – that's *Palm* Springs to you, although you probably thought I meant the bed springs, which I happen to love, too! And I play tennis now and try to keep a tan so I'm no longer that attractive shade of bleu cheese I used to be in New York! And I watch my diet and work out in a gym...

KIT. Christ, you really know you're in Hollywood when you see Jews with muscles!

(**MANNY** *picks up the shocking pink Christmas tree and hurls it across the room. It hits the wall, shattering the few pink ornaments.)*

KIT. That was too good for it!

MANNY. *(heatedly)* You think you can reach me but you can't! You think *you* like privacy! HA! All you know how to do is crawl into a hole. I know how to crawl into myself. You know how to hide out, I know how to *deaden* out! So I never have to feel that awful feeling of what it is to be alive!

KIT. *(calmly)* For a person who doesn't like confrontations, you certainly have changed, too.

MANNY. Yeah, and my hands are shaking and my head is pounding and I feel like my hair's on fire!

KIT. *You, you, you!* Do you ever read a book or a newspaper? Do you know what's going on in the world except what's going on with *you*?! Do you ever discuss anything? And I don't mean talk about yourself. You are, without a doubt, the most selfish, self-involved, self-absorbed son-of-a-bitch I have ever known. It's a wonder you aren't cross-eyed from contemplating your navel!

MANNY. And you! Giving of your perfect self to the point of treachery! It's impossible to live with a goddamn saint!

KIT. *(lightly)* I think it's time to swim ashore.

*(**KIT** starts for the stairs. **MANNY** stops her.)*

MANNY. You set standards no one can live up to! You guarantee it that you're going to be let down, betrayed. It's built-in from the start. Somebody's got to fall short of the mark sometime and when they do, *look out!* You're just sitting there, primed to be devastated – to take it personally!

KIT. I don't know where I got the idea that if you don't allow someone to shit all over you, you're being rude.

*(**KIT** goes up the stairs…)*

MANNY. Where're you going?

KIT. To bed. Alone. And you, Manny, *quo vadis?*

MANNY. *(after a moment)* I'm circlin' the drain. Without you, I'm going nowhere.

KIT. *(continuing)* Well, I'm traveling light. I'm going back to the back woods of Connecticut – back where I belong.

MANNY. *(runs to the railing)* Oh, Kit, come back to *me!* You don't have to leave tomorrow…wait…stay…stay with *me!* Live with me! Marry me again!

*(**KIT** stops, turns back to **MANNY**.)*

MANNY. I'll die if we don't get back together. Without you, I'll wither up and blow away.

KIT. You might think you will, but you won't. That's how I always felt when the Wall-Of-Silence got built – panicked that I was going to fall apart if I wasn't able to pull you back. But I survived. And you will, too. You'll get through.

(She turns and goes up a few stairs, but he grabs her hand over the railing.)

MANNY. But I've *changed*, Kit! And I want to change more! The only thing that hasn't *changed* is that I still love you.

KIT. *(sincerely)* And I still love you, Manny. And I always will. But sometimes love just isn't enough.

*(**MANNY** releases her hand.)*

I have to try too hard with you. There ought to be some little something that just naturally comes from loving someone – some gentle, effortless benefit – something that innately, ineffably enriches – that is graciously given on its own. It shouldn't have to be such hard work *all* the time. So relentlessly uphill. So patently unrewarding. Something must be shared – a thought, a laugh, half the weary load. I've changed, too, Manny. And not just my clothes.

MANNY. *(a bit stunned)* Oh, I can see that. I can *really* see that. But, Kit, some things about you I hope will never change.

KIT. Like?

MANNY. Like the way you watch me – when I'm talking to another woman, or when I'm kissing the children goodnight. There's that split second glance that lets me know there's something special that goes on with no one else but the two of us. I treasure that conspiracy.

KIT. *(softly)* I treasure it, too.

MANNY. Would someone else ever understand that?

KIT. Not *our* secret. But with someone else, perhaps we'd have a new and special secret with them.

MANNY. Yeah, but it wouldn't be as terrific as ours.

KIT. Who can say? I would hope so. The Other Woman and The Other Man are not necessarily out of the question. And they're not necessarily just jerks or fools.

MANNY. Wendy is no fool but she's out of the question! And Nick *is* a jerk, and he's absolutely out of the question!

KIT. And you and I are out of the question. And no two jerks have acted more foolishly than we have, and there's no question that we love each other – it's just an unworkable love. And we both have to face it.

(**KIT** *starts to go, but* **MANNY** *immediately speaks, stopping her one more time:*)

MANNY. I talked to Josh.

KIT. *(quietly)* Thank you. I'm proud of you. I really am, Manny. I know it wasn't easy for you.

(**MANNY** *nods modestly, pleased that he has pleased her…*)

MANNY. *(earnestly)* Come on, now, Kit, gimme a "Y," gimme an "E," gimme an "S-Oh-S"! Oh, Kit, I'll be there for you! With *balloons*, if you like. With a *band*! with *bells*! Ring-ring-ring!!

(The doorbell begins to ring…)

MANNY. *(nonplussed)* Who the hell is *that?*

KIT. Well, it's about a year too early for Santa.

MANNY. *(fuming, crosses to door)* Well, if it's fucking Father Time, his timing is shit, too! I know who it is! Mr. Half-The-Weary-Load!!

KIT. You mean, Colin???

(**MANNY** *tears open the front door to reveal* **NICK**…)

NICK. Kit!

KIT. NICK!!!

MANNY. Oh, my god, it's "Good Goods"!!! *(hysterically)* Go-back-go-back – go-back!!!

(**MANNY** *immediately ties to slam the door but* **NICK** *steps in and is half caught with* **MANNY** *wildly pushing it against him.* **NICK** *starts to yell and force the door back…*)

KIT. *(racing down the stairs) Manny, stop! You're hurting him!*

MANNY. *I'm trying to KILL him!*

(**KIT** *runs to tug at* **MANNY** *long enough for* **NICK** *to recover and push the door back forcefully, sending both* **KIT** *and* **MANNY** *to the floor.* **NICK** *rushes to* **KIT**…)

NICK. *(realizes what he's done)* Ohh, Kit, I'm sorry! Are you hurt?!

(NICK helps her up. MANNY is scrambling to his feet…)

KIT. What are you doing here? I just got balloons from you!

(MANNY fiercely grabs the huge bouquet of balloons, hopelessly tangling himself in the strings as he smashes them, kicks them, stomps them…)

MANNY. Yeah, here, take these fucking things and go round the world in them!!!

NICK. *(re: MANNY)* I knew he was going to do something tricky so I knew I had to do something tricky, too!!!

MANNY. GET-OUT-GET-OUT-GET-OUT!!!

(MANNY, tangled in the balloons, comes at NICK again, tackles him and they tumbles into the "bouquet," popping the balloons like firecrackers with their weight…)

KIT. Oh, Manny, stop it!! Both of you, stop it!!!

(KIT now helps NICK to his feet while MANNY remains more ensnarled than ever…)

NICK. Kit, come with me! I've got a taxi waiting outside!

MANNY. *(condescendingly)* A *taxi*?! How very "old money" of you!

NICK. *(to KIT)* Please, darling!

KIT. Oh, Nick, I can't. Besides, there's not a flight till morning. The kids and I are already booked on it!

NICK. I've chartered a plane to take us all to Palm Springs!

MANNY. Oh, so you like the Springs, too!

NICK. *(to KIT, intensely)* We can be married there. We can have our honeymoon there. Start the New Year there. Our new life together!

KIT. Oh, Nick, I can't! Can't you see I can't?

NICK. I'll wait outside till you pack. Till you and the kids get ready!

KIT. *(after a moment, simply)* I can't because I don't love you.

(Silence. MANNY watches them breathlessly…)

NICK. *(crestfallen)* Well, that *does* make a difference. It doesn't make it impossible, it just makes a difference.

KIT. Oh, Nick, you don't want *me*. You'll meet someone else. You've had so many wives, I know you can find one more.

NICK. What are you *talking* about?! I've been married *once*!

KIT. But you were engaged to those others.

NICK. *Others*? I've been engaged twice. Once to the woman I married and once to you!

MANNY. Well, that's *plural*! So that's *others*!

(**KIT** *takes off the diamond earrings…*)

KIT. Nick, you're a wonderful person. Better than all of us. My mother loves you.

MANNY. Yeah, so why don't you marry her mother?

NICK. *(directly to* **MANNY***)* Because I don't love her mother!

MANNY. Well, neither do I.

KIT. And neither do I. Well, I love her and I hate her, if you know what I mean.

MANNY. *(to* **NICK,** *shrugs)* Yeah, the usual.

KIT. *(sincerely, to* **NICK***)* You have no idea how truly sorry I am that this couldn't work out…but it would be a mistake. It would be a lie.

NICK. A lie?

KIT. *(nods)* Well, I know I'd be lying to myself. And I don't ever want to lie to you − *(quickly)* or to myself, if I can help it. *(puts the earrings in his hand)* I hope this new year holds for you…all the things you deserve. But I know I'm not one of them.

NICK. Do you love Manny?

(**KIT** *looks at* **MANNY**. *He returns her look expectantly.*)

KIT. Yes. I always have and I always will. But it was a mistake to marry him, too, and I'll never, ever make that mistake again.

(**MANNY**'*s face sags.*)

MANNY. *(swallows dryly)* I'm dehydrated.

NICK. I'm not surprised. All that foaming at the mouth.

(**NICK** *looks at* **KIT** *a long moment, turns and silently goes out.* **KIT** *slowly closes the door.* **MANNY** *quickly goes to the bar, quickly pours himself a glass of champagne, chug-a-lugs it.*)

(**KIT** *crosses to the stairs and begins to ascend them again...*)

MANNY. *(turning)* Kit, wait! Listen to me!! I'll try to open up and you try to be less perfect. Now I ask you, what could beat that combination?

KIT. *(stops; sweetly and directly)* Nothing.

MANNY. Yeah, *nothing!*

KIT. But let's be honest. Even at that, do you know what hell it would be?

MANNY. I'm afraid I do.

KIT. I'm afraid I do, too. Goodnight, Manny. And, once more with feeling...goodbye.

(**KIT** *smiles at him, turns and goes up the rest of the stairs and off.*)

(**MANNY** *watches her until she is gone. He turns away from the stairs, facing the audience, trying to think what to do. Suddenly, he goes to the phone, punches a number, and while it's ringing, he consults a telephone book.*)

MANNY. *(into phone)* Music Express? Charlie? Yeah, hi, it's Manny, happy New Year! Listen, I want to cancel a limo I booked for tomorrow morning to take my family to the airport. No, they're not going. Decided they like it here so much they're gonna stay. Yeah, how about that! Yeah, thanks a lot. – *(Hangs up. Referring to number in phone book, punching it into phone:)* Hello, American Airlines? I want to cancel a reservation for three on your eight a.m. flight to New York. Sure, I'll hold on. You never talked to anybody who'd be so thrilled to hold on.

(**MANNY** *smiles to himself...*)

Curtain

Connecticut Farm

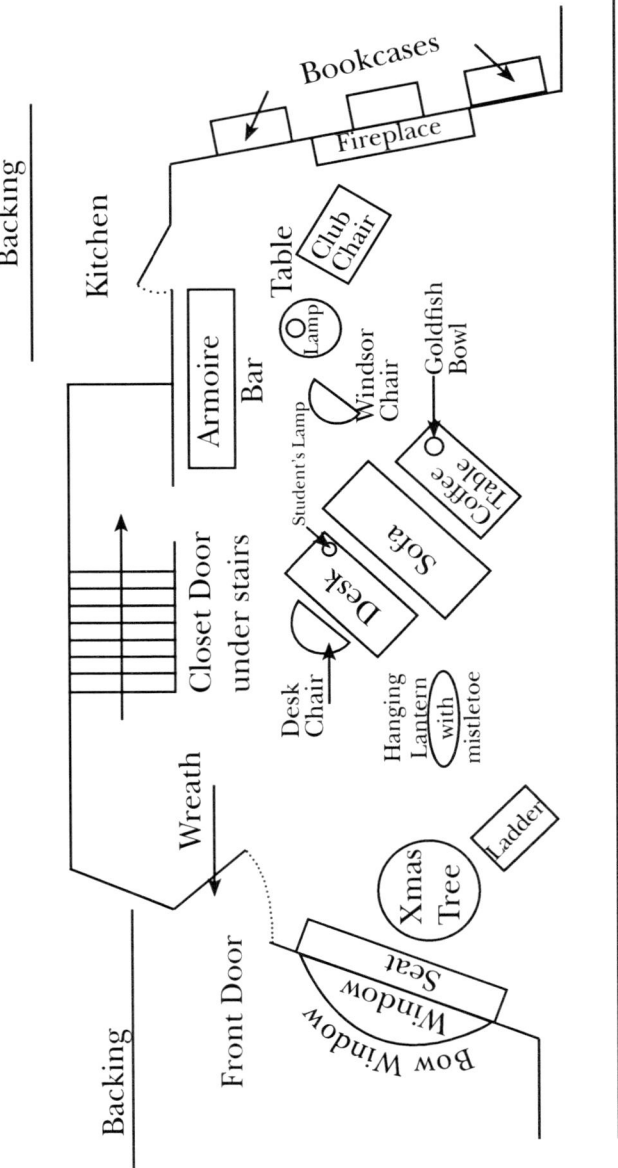

Backing

Bookcases

Fireplace

Kitchen

Table

Club Chair

Armoire

Bar

Lamp

Windsor Chair

Student's Lamp

Goldfish Bowl

Coffee Table

Closet Door under stairs

Desk

Sofa

Desk Chair

Hanging Lantern with mistletoe

Wreath

Ladder

Xmas Tree

Front Door

Bow Window

Window Seat

Backing

Avec Schmaltz
Act One

Avec Schmaltz
California Spanish-Style Living Room

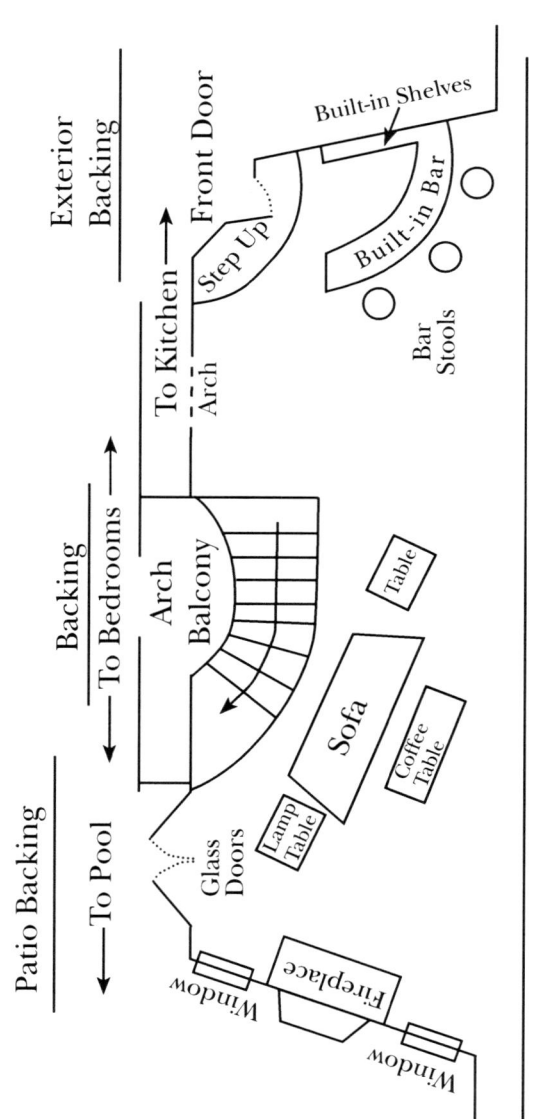

Exterior Backing

Front Door

Built-in Shelves

Step Up

Built-in Bar

Bar Stools

To Kitchen
Arch

Backing

To Bedrooms

Arch
Balcony

Table

Sofa

Coffee Table

Lamp Table

Patio Backing

To Pool

Glass Doors

Window

Fireplace

Window

Act Two

Also by
Mart Crowley...

The Boys in the Band

A Breeze From the Gulf

For Reasons that Remain Unclear

The Men from the Boys

Remote Asylum

OTHER TITLES AVAILABLE FROM SAMUEL FRENCH

REMOTE ASYLUM

Mart Crowley

Drama / 5m, 3f

In the heat of a blazing summer, three physically and spiritually exhausted Americans: Tom, a famous tennis pro, Dinah, his beautiful, cosmopolitan, not-yet-divorced lover, and their mutual pal, Michael, a gay writer (first introduced in *The Boys in the Band*), try to "get away from it all" by visiting Dinah's enormously wealthy retired friends - the older, imperious Irene and her terminally ill husband, Ray - at their fabulous cliff-side villa on an island in the Mediterranean. But it turns out to be far from the perfect, restorative holiday they were so desperately seeking. This odyssey has not brought them or their hosts anywhere near the paradise they were seeking, but rather to an inferno where a painful, purgatorial breakthrough occurs, releasing them all and providing true escape from this distant and deceptively idyllic haven. Remote Asylum is a play which observes the classical unities of time, place and action, which remorselessly exposes a group of bruised souls - wanderers all, and forces them to deal with their fears of loneliness and mortality, to open past emotional wounds not yet healed. The event is one of forceful, dynamic trans- figuration; the conversation is intelligent and adult, both witty and grave, best described as a kind of orchestrated tone poem.

Lightning Source UK Ltd.
Milton Keynes UK
20 November 2010

163150UK00001B/4/P